# *Folklore, Faerie, Enchantment, & Real Life*

By
Christian Ifayomi

PublishAmerica
Baltimore

First printing





ISBN: 1-60703-845-5
PUBLISHED BY PUBLISHAMERICA, LLLP
www.publishamerica.com
Baltimore

Printed in the United States of America

This book is dedicated to my family: Dorothy, Alvin, Sarah and Johannes. Because of their patience and understanding throughout the long years of my trying to be an author.

# Acknowledgments

To my siblings, their spouses and all those (Editors, Teachers, Relatives and Friends) who through out these trying years gave me their moral, financial and editing support and other encouragements on my writings.

# *Folklore, Faerie, Enchantment, & Real Life*

# An Infernal Death

Three days; days of ecstatic and unparalleled bliss flew by in which, Roberts, Alex—Inspector, Sierra Leone Police—enjoyed special favors from the woman he'd craved. He'd arrived in the capital, Freetown, two years earlier and fell immediately under her spell at a reception in Bo. Lying next to her their bodies intimately touching he examined hers: Naked, full-bosomed, ebony skinned; he marveled at its contrast to his.

His right hand moved from his stomach to her right breast and gently began massaging its pliant nipple. He whimpered as that organ hardened under his fingers:

She moaned, twisted around to face him and her lips parted inviting in his tongue; she sucked at it her teeth caressing it eliciting a sigh from him.

Grabbing his manhood, she ran a nail along its length and when it became more turgid, bent down and shoved it into her mouth:

Bullets of air blasted from his flaring nostrils as her tongue slowly teased the organ and she slobbered all over it.

He brought her head up, put his mouth to a breast to massage its nipple with a vibrant tongue. Straddling her, his buttocks became the powerhouse as his penis acted as the piston which gave both unthinkable and blinding pleasures.

At the end, they laid spent breath wheezing from open mouths. Lucky, lucky man, he thought smiling. This is the one woman that can quench my sexual fires and we have been at it for the past three days. Wow! Talk about variety: There was no position in or form of sex they had not tried. His smile became more impish: To think my wife believes I am on inspection in Makeni.

"A penny for them," the voice of Memona, his companion, broke into his thoughts. "You've been too quiet during the past five minutes."

"Oh, it's nothing," he said. "Before leaving London, friends told me that women here were easy to come by: 'Some perfume, a few yards of cotton material and they'll be all over you, even murder someone for you, they said,' forgetting to talk about the pleasure."

"You know better, now, huh?" She asked. "I wondered why you showered me with all those gifts. One mustn't believe everything one is told, more so about Sierra Leonean women. You realize that now, right?"

He nodded. The first time he'd laid eyes on her had been at an official banquet in the Bo Town Community Center for the visit of the President of the Gambia. Blood had rushed to his penis causing an embarrassing erection. He'd wanted to die. He was fortunate his wife wasn't there with him.

"Liar," she nestled closer to him.

"That's the truth. I could have taken you at that very moment. You had on superfluous yellow attire—gown, fabulous headgear, and lappa—that made your behind behave like an elephant wrapped in an ice-cold, wet blanket. You turned me on, woman. But, being the wife of the Chairman, Bo Town Council, I couldn't approach you then, could I?"

"Why? Not? So that's why you started sending cards and all those expensive gifts, huh?"

He hadn't the nerve to approach her while the Chairman lived: He and her husband were good friends. His sudden death, however, made there being together possible. He was a lucky, lucky, man? Wasn't he?"

She rose on her right elbow to look into his face. There was talk of her husband being killed by the police. He must have heard something about that? Were the police going to investigate the matter, further? Find out who did him in?

"Nah," he said. "You saw the corpse? His death was caused by some wild animal. The investigations put it on a leopard or tiger. Why did he go hunting alone? Couldn't he take a few men for protection?"

She rested her head on his chest and giggled.

"He liked playing the hero; at seventy-three, you'd think he'd given up things like hunting by himself and marrying women fifty years younger than he was. But enough of that, did you need a year to approach me after his death?" She asked. "Man, for a police officer, you sure lack self-esteem."

He sped from the bed to slap on the clothes he picked from the floor.

"How should I have known you were interested in me?" He asked. "You returned all the presents I sent you—unopened—when I first saw you."

She sat at the edge of the bed her feet swinging forward and backward like a pendulum, as he dressed. A girl doesn't have to give in too easily; it would make a man consider her a floozy. The wait did both of them good: She took the time to grieve without people talking and his love continued to grow while he waited.

He would never think of her as a floozy he protested, took her into his arms and kissed her. It was time for the past to be forgotten. He hoped they continued to have good times, like these, forever.

He left for Freetown on the Saturday bearing Object-de-art, live poultry (chickens and ducks) and tons of fresh fruits for his un-suspecting family.

Standing at the head of their dinner table—carving implements in hand—the following Sunday the lewd love-making scenes at Memona's contrasted with that of the domestic bliss that was supposed to be at play before him: Give him the former any day he thought. God, he missed her: Correctly, her buttocks as they wriggled in her tightly tied lappa and the bounce of bare breasts as she walked about the house half naked on most occasions. But mostly, he missed his erect member's thrusting motions into her warm, moist, and grasping pussy and the pure delight that brought him.

To hide an erection, he stabbed at the chicken in front of him: Bright red blood trickled out of the cut to flow unto and stain the white charger the bird was presented on.

Damn you, woman, he thought, this bird isn't completely cooked. His face clouded over with rage and his hands trembled allowing the carving utensils to crash to the floor.

"What's the matter, dear?" His spouse asked her voice reaching him from afar. "You've gone as white as a Tide-washed sheet."

She rose and walked to where he stood.

He said nothing was the matter. They must continue with their dinner and not wait for him. He, however, took care not to eat the flesh of the bird but had a bowl of dessert instead. One's imagination sure plays tricks on one he thought looking at the charger: Blood still oozed from the bird. Was he the only one in the room who saw it? He wondered watching the others tuck into the bird. Am I going crazy? He'd better see his medic soonest.

Thoughts of his stay with Memona and their wanton lovemaking, however, drove the incident from his mind.

Perusing a manual, three weeks later, he heard some rushing sounds in his office: Since they came from the ceiling, he stood on a chair and with the help of his baton banged on it thinking, maybe, there were rats.

He gasped, almost falling off the chair as blood stained the spot he'd struck. He watched, mesmerized, as it quickly expanded. He came off the chair and went to his seat. The next time he looked up, the stain had advanced to the walls to his right and left and slender tendrils were snaking their way down them.

Anxiously watching the tendrils, something forced him to the wall to his left and, with the use of a chair, trailed his baton along one of the tendrils. It erupted showering the baton and his trembling fingers with its cloying contents. He began to shake and could feel the blood vessels at his temples thumping madly. A construction jackhammer pumped in the place of his heart and a burning and tingling sensation, starting at the fingers, rapidly made its way up his arm.

"Help," he shouted falling off the chair and whimpering.

His office door flew open and a sergeant rushed in:

"You called for help, sir?" She asked. "Is anything the matter with you?"

"Nothing, sergeant," her superior answered as he rose. "I fell while investigating something on that wall. Do you see anything, but my certificates, on it?"

"I don't sir," she said. "I had this office cleaned while you were in Makeni, sir. "The Boss' office shouldn't look like a dump, I said to myself when I did so."

The fallen man staggered to his chair.

"Don't be impertinent and rude, sergeant," he said as he sat down. "Go to your cubicle and stay there. Haven't you some work to do?"

He wondered if he was really going mad after the sergeant left. The tingling sensation in his arm—which had slowly moved up to his elbow—was soon forgotten as the days flew by and he began preparing for another visit to his heart's desire.

This time around, he told the department and his family that he had some inspection to make in the division based in Sulima. Everything went well until the day he arrived at Bo and he and Memona rested, in their sweat, after a long bout of sex.

"Do you see something on the ceiling, dear?" He asked suddenly sitting up. "It's racing for the wall facing the foot of the bed."

He felt sweat pour out of his twitching face as the tingling sensation that started in his office, returned.

"Look," he said, when she rose and bit his ear, "It is flowing down all four walls, now. Don't you see it, love? Am I going crazy? Am I the only one seeing these things?"

Memona stared intently at the four walls and the ceiling.

"What's the matter with you?" She asked. "There's nothing but pictures and the ceiling rose on them. Maybe, you were dreaming; pull yourself together, man."

She watched him slide beneath the blanket then pull it over his head.

"Come on love," she said, "Share what's bothering you. I want to help."

"Are you looking for something to laugh at?" He asked his head reappearing.

"The look on your face tells me it must be something serious," she said. "Come out with it."

"For the months we've been going together," he said thinking it wouldn't do any harm telling her of his experiences, "I've seen blood flow from the ceiling of rooms I am in. It descends the walls then heads for me. It started when having dinner with my family after I returned home the last time I visited you."

"Must be your imagination," she said. "What happens next and why does it affect you so much?"

The next time it happened—in his office in Freetown—he'd touched one of the tendrils; it exploded and spilled its contents all over his arm leaving a tingling sensation in it. Now, those tendrils are for ever getting closer to wherever he is and he was afraid they would one day engulf him. He stopped talking; she'd burst out laughing.

"Don't tell me you've become superstitious," she said. "It's all in your mind, dear, that, or you've begun doing drugs. I know you're not drunk."

"I tell you there's blood cascading down walls and heading for me bent on devouring me and all you do is laugh and think I'm on drugs?" He asked. "Woman, I have never done drugs in my life and I won't start doing it now. Never have, never will."

She apologized. She had to laugh, she said, even though she hadn't meant to be flippant: He would have laughed too if he could have seen his face: The fear and consternation in it.

"I thought you'd seen a ghost. Have you spoken to a Psychiatrist?"

He jumped off the bed to get a glass of cold water from the kitchen.

"I haven't but I'll do so the minute I get back to Freetown," he said on his return. "All he'll do is prescribe some medication and tell me to take a rest. What good will that do to a-so-called-hallucination?"

He put the glass on a side table and went over to kiss her on the cheek. He was grabbed around the neck, his head pulled closer to hers, and his lips passionately kissed.

Standing on rubbery legs he heard her say,

"Come to bed, Lover boy. Don't dwell too long on such problems: They usually find ways of solving themselves with time."

He lost it: She'd stuck her wet tongue into his ear and wiggled it around. Hot stabs of unmitigated lust ravished his frame and his member stood at attention.

She bit his left earlobe: He groaned as wave after wave of feelings rushed up his trembling limbs heading for the erect organ. He fell into the bed and soon had her panting in unison with him. A finger slid, slowly, into his bum hole: He farted. When it made circular movements within it, he couldn't wait and shot hot, gooey sperm all over her glistering body.

"You couldn't wait, could you?" She asked.

"Whose fault was it? He replied. "Never do that to me if you want to be completely satisfied."

Lying spent, each finally knew where the others vulnerable spots were: They realized it would be a race to see who would make the other come the earliest.

During the heat of such passionate lovemaking over the next five days, sights of blood scurrying across ceilings and walls were pushed into the dark recesses of his mind.

He returned to the capital at the end of this period and the tingling sensations, to arms and other body parts, returned as did blood rushing down walls: He visited his physician.

Looking up at the ceiling, from the physician's examination table, he screamed his eyes widening with fear,

"There Doc, above your head, can't you see it?"

"See what and where?" The doctor asked.

"Blood," he said. "It's flowing down the wall behind you. There, it just engulfed your diplomas."

The poor man turned to face the wall behind him.

"I see no blood," he said after a while, "and my diplomas are just fine. Young man, you are distraught; we must do some tests after which you'll have to see a Psychiatrist."

His patient rushed to his feet.

"Tests, tests that is all you ever talk about, Doctor. There are tendrils, from a stream of bright red blood, embedding themselves in your carpet; I want you to do something about that, I don't want to do any stupid tests. Those will only cost me time and money"

The medic walked over to put an arm about his shoulders.

"The tests will give me some ideas about what your condition is," he said. "Take these prescriptions for the next two weeks. If the hallucinations continue, come back and see me; we'll do the tests then."

"Just as I thought: Nothing but medications. Give them to me," he said snatching the prescriptions from him. With a last frightened look at what he thought was soaking its way toward him he scuttled out of the room shouting incoherently.

A night later, he awoke screaming,

"Help, dear, help me," his legs pounding the mattress under the bed covers, "Blood is engulfing my legs."

His spouse awoke to find that his face was covered with fear, pain, and sweat. She got up, searched in the bathroom, for a towel, returned with one to gently wipe his perspiring face and body down.

"Is anything wrong with you, dear?" She asked testing where he indicated the pajamas clung to his legs. "You shouted something about blood creeping up your legs: I think you perspired on them. That's no reason to be afraid, love. You are in our bedroom, on your bed and you are sleeping with, me, your wife. Go back to sleep."

"I tell you, woman, my legs are awash in the vile fluid. I can feel its cloying warmth creeping up my thighs."

She grabbed the covers and threw them off his legs:

His legs were completely dry.

"There's nothing the matter with your legs," she said replacing the covers. "A vivid imagination is your real problem. What's happening to you?"

"The past weeks," he began after a long silence.

"I mean before that," she said. "This didn't start four weeks ago, start at the beginning."

"You don't want to know about that, love," he said shaking his head. "You'll end up hurt."

"Try me and see. I'll try my best to understand."

"You know that the Chairman Bo Town Council got killed some months ago?" He said. "Well, it wasn't done by wild animals. I had some of my men kill him."

"Why would you want the Councilman murdered?" She asked when she got her breath back. "Did you know him that well? I don't think so."

"I didn't know him that well. I met his wife at that banquet, in Bo, for the Gambian President, and immediately wanted her, badly; she became an obsession."

He rose up to his waist and reached for her hand, again, when she began to sob quietly and slowly rock her body both arms tightly wrapped around her shoulders.

"You're saying you had an affair with a Native, black woman? Don't you dare touch me," she barked removing her hand and sitting up in bed tears flowing down her face to splash on the cotton sheets and covers.

He nodded yes.

"And, for nearly a year, you slept with me too? Bastard! God, what a fool I have been."

He tried going after her; she'd gone to sit in a chair a few feet away from the bed. I should take her in my arms and kiss her he thought but moving was a problem: His legs were pinned down by some unseen weight.

"It wasn't for a year, dear," he said. "I began seeing her about two months ago."

"Was that because she rejected your advances when her spouse was alive? And were those 'Going on Inspection Trips' just to be with her?"

He said yes feeling the warm sticky fluid creeping up his sides.

"Love, I realize that what I did was wrong. Please, please forgive me."

Her body language said otherwise.

"Ah-h-h, it's pressing on my chest; I can't breathe," he wheezed as he fought to take in air. "Help me, dear. For heavens sake, don't just sit there and watch me die, call for an ambulance. If not, get our doctor to see me here at home."

She made herself more comfortable in the chair as he watched. Supporting her head in her cupped hands, she said,

"Mr. Mustapha must be exacting payment for his death, at long last. Myself, I wouldn't have minded if she were European or even Lebanese. But a Native; what has she got that I haven't? I see; she's got bigger tits and a behind one could lose oneself in; also, she showed you some liberated ways of making love, huh? And, in due time, they would have been introduced to me, not so?"

She got up and sped to the bed.

"Bastard: You bastard." She sobbed her fists pummeling his chest. "I hate you, oh, how I hate you. Of all the things to do to me, you went with a Native whore. God, if you weren't slowly dying, I'd send you off to your grave."

She pried loose the hands that tried to hold her to him.

"Dear, forgive me," he begged. "Be an angel and forgive me, love?"

He could feel the fluid rise up his extended arms as trails of hot tears flowed down his face.

"Be a Christian my darling," he said. "Have pity on a dying man and call our doctor; I swear I'll make it up to you in whatever way you wish."

"Servers you right," she said shaking her head "There's nothing anyone can do for you now. In God's and our communities' eyes, you are a murderer. To commit adultery with the murdered man's spouse makes your actions reprehensible. I'll see that you rot in hell for the hurt and hard times this family will go through after you're dead. You won't be screwing damned Natives where you're going; you can bet on that."

The blood was at his throat and was climbing rapidly. Soon, it was up to his chin and at the lower lip.

"Help me, dear: If not for mine then for the sakes of the God you worship and our young children. Who'd look after you and the kids after I'm gone?" He lipped.

"The God who took care of us while you were ravishing your whore in Bo," she said, "He will."

There were gurgling noises; blood gushed into his mouth and poured down his throat heading for the stomach. He endured three full minutes of the rancid taste then the vile fluid crept—ever-so-slowly—upward, to his nostrils.

I love you he thought. Pity you couldn't see your way into giving me another chance at living. He shuddered as the menacing tendrils inched into his nostrils then, sensing victory, stampeded in making him gasp for breath, choking him.

He tried to vomit his eyes closing, involuntarily, but the loathsome fluid quickly invaded his tired lungs.

The autopsy, later that week, said he drowned in—of all things—his own blood.

# Unraveling Friendship

The earth rested her battles with the scorching sun over for the day. She released her entrapped magma like heat into the cool, evening atmosphere above. Along the River Rokel—Sierra Leone's most picturesque—fireflies danced to the songs of melodious bullfrogs and crickets. On the east bank, Manso relaxed enjoying the spectacular beauty of his surroundings and the gentle breeze, impregnated with the perfumed smells of moss and decay, wafting its way leisurely from across the river.

He listened as the buzzing of cowboy mosquitoes, riding the crest of the breeze, rivaled the solemn voice of a Muezzin calling the faithful to worship. Slapping at these pests, he followed the floater bobbing its way down river and gloried at the wavering pattern the dying rays of the sun made on the shimmering surface of the water.

He wondered if he should have gone to prayers. That would have pleased his father very much, but papa had not lived in Freetown with him.

Shifting on his stone seat, he tugged on the line then focused on the swaying palm trees on the opposite bank.

"Give me just one for my effort," he prayed looking upwards. "One to show Abu I'm still a better fisherman than him."

He took a swig from the bully of palm wine by his side.

The beats of bats' wings, as they plunged into the insects attracted by his burn-fire, rudely interrupted his thoughts. Shooing them away, he chuckled over what had transpired between Abu and himself earlier that day. He'd asked as they drank in a palm-wine bar, if they had decided to initiate him into their Sokoh Society.

"Nah," Abu said. "Others are in no hurry to decide. You wait for many years after the entry age, before you apply. Two more months won' kill you."

Where did he stand he'd asked. He would need his help if he was to become a member.

"With them," Abu replied. "We won' hurry, because you have School Leaving Certificate. That does not get you into the society quickly."

Hiding his hurt and disappointment, Manso invited him to go fishing some evening, soon. He reminded him of the times (when younger) during which they stole from their homes to do that.

His friend took a long sip from his palm wine cup, wiped the sweat from his face then smiled.

"I do remember," he said. "But I work late on my farm now. Beside, the fishes have gone from the river and people don't fish during the day let—alone in the evenings—any more."

"Come on," his friend replied. "You can leave the farm early on that day. You can't go on working at the pace you are."

Their eyes locked. Abu wiped the froth from his lips. He no longer fished he said. Strange things happened to those who did: Especially those who fished at night.

His friend laughed and told him not to be an old woman. If he was afraid, he could take a weapon or his spouse, to hold his hands, along."

A light flashed in Abu's eyes when he heard him out but he remained calm, gulped down his drink, rose and walked leisurely out of the bar.

By the meandering river, Manso focused on his fishing as the feathery fingers of a burst of playfully hot wind, from across river, caressed his face. He loved fishing along the Rokel River's bank. It had not been the same fishing the Atlantic Ocean in Freetown: There he'd spent most of his evenings sitting on stones on Mount Aureole watching ships sail bye on the ocean and the lights of vehicles twinkling, way down below, in the city's narrow streets.

Fifteen years of that life passed before he returned home. Everything had changed: The most annoying being his one-time friends—especially Abu—looking on him as an 'Opoto,' a White man.

He relaxed as he watched his floater ride the current further down stream. Coming home, to Lunsar, had been a disturbing experience. He'd arrived with the idea of ultimately becoming a Town Councilor. This would be the vehicle that would take him to the National Parliament in Freetown; he couldn't do this without his friends' help.

Rapidly approaching footsteps, above the chirps and buzzing of the insects, reached him and he listened intently. They were footsteps all right: They came from the brushes to his left. He froze not daring to breathe. All went quiet around him.

"It must be my imagination," he said breathing normally again. "Maybe, it was the breeze rushing through the brushes."

He took a swig from his bully (gourd) of palm wine to wet his suddenly parched throat. "I'll fish until eight-thirty; I'll hate to face Abu, if I reel in nothing," he said.

He was about to take another pull from the bully when the

sounds of approaching footsteps recurred. For one second, he thought they were human but listening closely, he concluded they were not friends trying to scare him shitless. He decided they were those of a heavy animal that was scurrying toward him.

What animal would be so heavy yet move that fast? He thought.

A sudden tug on the line and thoughts of disembodied sounds were erased from his mind. Judging from the wash of the water, the catch was a huge one: His heart went racing. He finally reeled it in after a long hard fight. He had it up in the air and was examining it, with the aid of his helmet lamp, when sharp claws tore into his right shoulder.

He let the fish fall as he turned to face the danger: A huge crocodile, on its hind legs, stood behind him. A wave of vile-smelling breath washed over his face; the head—a dribbling vise—had drawn closer to his person. The red bolt-like eyes, at the vise's hinges, stared malevolently at him. He raised an arm for protection only to have it savaged by the creature's saliva dripping teeth.

A chunk of flesh came off the raised arm causing him excruciating pain while his uninjured left arm beat feebly on the leathery skin of the incensed animal.

The crazed reptile's attention was soon drawn to the fish flopping about and gasping on the ground. While it was so engaged, he ran for his life.

Why was the creature's skin so dry? He wondered as he underwent treatment on the injured arm at Lunsar's General Hospital. He needed answers to this and some other questions that bothered him as he lay in bed in a ward.

Superstition said that people sometimes assumed animal forms to get at their enemies. Was this one of those occasions? But, that was crap: He didn't believe it as a child and scoffed and laughed at it now he had his School Leaving Certificate.

"I cannot think of a reason for a crocodile's attack on me," he informed Morlai, his Dad, who with Abu visited him the next day in the hospital. "Dad, can animals walk on their hind legs?" He asked.

Not if they were real wild animals, was the answer. It may have been taught how if it was tamed. People, however, become raging beasts sometimes and supposedly walk on their hind legs when they attack those they hate.

"Who would want to hurt me? Everyone is so friendly: They say they are happy to have me back."

"Why do they attack you then?" Abu asked.

"You must be careful when you fish in the evenings," his Dad said.

His friend wanted to know why he should fish in the evenings at all. Could he not fish in the afternoons like everybody else? They waited for an answer but none came.

"If you insist on fishing in the evenings, take a weapon with you," Morlai said. "I'll give you—"

"The witchdoctor say that normal bullets won' hurt these animals," Abu butted in. "A gun need special bullets to destroy such creatures."

His friend laughed; it ended in a cough.

"Bet you get those from our esteemed witchdoctor, huh? What does he do with them? Fill them up with human dung?"

Another light flashed in Abu's eyes.

"You mock our ways, not so?" He asked his hands rolled tightly by his sides. "One day soon, you will understand that your book learning don' explain all in our world."

"I will take the gun, Dad," the patient said shaking his head. "Please, no special bullets; it's all hogwash: Believed only by fools and old feeble women."

He laughed.

"Thic, thic, Abu, you are something else. If you must know, my book learning can explain most anything. Give me enough time, and I will unravel most of what passes for mystery in this place."

His Dad looked over at Abu then laid his hand on his son's bandaged arm.

"Didn't say nothing 'bout special bullets, son," he said tapping the arm. "Don't mock our ways; they were here long before the White-man—and his learning—came. They will go on long after he leave."

"Dad, they do not believe in all that nonsense. They make fun of them,"

Morlai nodded and then smiled.

"How come they have words like 'ghosts' and the 'devil' in their language? How come some go to a 'Lodge' once a month?" He asked. "Why do they try to be members of our secret societies? There must be something in them that they want to learn. Take what is best from their teachings, son, but remember from where you came and who you really are."

The patient grimaced. He had not meant to offend. Turning to Abu, he asked if they were still debating his application into their society.

The latter shrugged. For somebody who no longer believed in their customs and ways, he was quite eager to enter their society, he said. The matter was out of his hands: Many others applied before him. A vote on his application would come after theirs. If he was elected into the society, he would eventually become PASHEA (ALL WISE HEAD) in a few years because of his education. Now, however, the society had to feel he was fit to be admitted.

"The society way for generations," Morlai said. He turned to Abu, "Come. We leave now. We must go before he become too excited."

His son spent a restful week recuperating in the hospital. On his discharge, he took to relaxing outdoors under the blazing sun. The third of these crazy carefree afternoons found him praying, that the rain threatening the brilliance of the sun would pass. He agonized over the fact that, if the droplets hitting the ground increased, he and his nephews and nieces would bake in their oven-like hut when they went in.

These thoughts soon evaporated when an ominous sound reached his ears: It came from beyond the hedges that surrounded the yard. He herded the kids in the direction of the hut as the head of a crocodile appeared in the enclave. Its bloodshot eyes roamed about and then locked on the group hurrying toward the building.

It charged making the group scurry forward causing a three-year-old boy to fall. Their pet dog gave assistance by enticing the beast away from him; it turned disastrous when it slipped and powerful jaws grabbed him about the middle, and shook him into two. It was then the turn of the fallen child who had gotten up and, on wobbly legs, hurried after his fleeing relatives. A few yards from safety, he fell again this time on his face.

Manso watched the animal and the child thrash about which finally caused the latter's right leg to come off. He pulled himself together, rushed the other kids into the house ran to his bedroom from where he retrieved a shotgun. He arrived by the bleeding child in a blinding rage.

The severed leg was down to the ankle in the creature's throat as he sent a stream of bullets into it; they bounced off its leathery skin. Trying to reload made him an easy target and as the distance between him and the animal decreased, he could smell its rabid breath. He realized he couldn't reload in time; the gun became a club.

Several massive blows later, the weapon's butt was destroyed but the monster abandoned its attack. Soon, gunshots and curses chased its retreating form as male relatives, with various weapons, joined in the fray.

At the hospital, Manso pondered the situation: Attacking a helpless, three-year-old boy and his pet was the most loathsome act anything could commit. Over the next week the child's stay in the hospital weighed on his mind. He blamed himself and the impotency of his bullets for the debacle. He worried over whether to purchase a new weapon with heavier munitions by the time the child came out of the danger-list.

What if those didn't work? Wouldn't that endanger his life? Discussions with his Dad brought up the idea of the witchdoctor's special bullets. For a full week, he quibbled. Only when told another attack might end in the gruesome demise of a close relative or himself did he take his Dad's advice.

Two visits to the witchdoctor were necessary before he was seen by that worthy; he was that busy. Something had attacked him by the river several weeks ago he began when asked what his problem was. Over a week ago, the same creature attacked his three-year-old nephew, and their pet, in the enclave of their home and ate his right leg; his shots had no effects on the animal.

"Why come to me?" The witchdoctor asked humming to himself.

His visitor asked if he wasn't a witchdoctor.

Smiling, his fingers working the cowry-shell rosary around his neck, his host said, "If I was you, I go leave Lunsar."

The visitor wondered why.

"Someone want you out of Lunsar; don't want you in the Sokoh Society."

The client pondered the information then asked for a name. If that wasn't forthcoming, he wanted some of his special bullets.

"With you learning, fine clothes, and motorbike," the former continued, "he say you make magic: Turn his woman's head."

Manso shrugged and asked when he could become a member of the esteemed society. He was told to go back to Freetown; he would never be a member of the society.

"This is my home," he protested. "I returned only to help my beloved town and Chiefdom. I won't flee to the capital."

His host demanded he be quiet.

"You want me special bullets?" He asked. "What type gun you shoot?"

He said a twelve-gauge shotgun.

"It will cost you," he said rising and hurrying to a back room to emerge a few minutes later with something wrapped in tattered and torn printed papers.

"Use these in gun," he said, handing him the parcel. "Shoot for the legs."

"Why mustn't I shoot at anywhere else? And what is the cost?"

"Allah, don't he understand?" He asked. "I said, shoot for the legs. Leave Lunsar, now. Something terrible will happen. I advise you because your father is my friend."

These warnings left the visitor shaken; he'd returned to Lunsar for specific reasons: To set up a head-quarter and to start campaigning for the next general elections. Nothing would make him leave before these were done.

Stopping at the Paterson Zochonis store, he bought a new twelve-gauge shotgun, fishing equipment and a container of bait.

Over a calabash of palm wine, at their usual watering hole, he bragged about his night fishing prowess and his hopes of beaching the greatest number of fishes when next he fished which he announced would be soon.

Friends—Abu most incessantly—cautioned against his going

fishing at night. A third encounter with his nemesis could be dangerous; he could be killed.

"Okay for you to talk." He replied. "You don't have to prove anything. You are an important member of your Society."

"Why must you prove anything to our Society?" Abu asked. "We didn't ask for proof."

"To show, I am still one of you; that I am worthy to be a member of your Society." Manso said taking a sip from his calabash.

His friend's brow knotted. That wasn't what kept him from entering; the members worried over his bringing the ways of the White-man into the society: The one-man-one vote nonsense. They loved the way; the society voted and how it operated: They loathed his democracy.

"I understand it is my education and possessions that are the roots of the problem," Manso said. "Schools have not closed down, yet, in Freetown."

"So?"

"You can still attend. Some of you," he eyed Abu, "were invited, no, begged to come to Freetown: You hadn't the balls; you preferred to hang around your mother's lappas."

"Didn't that make some of us PASHEA—which you want to be, now—many years ago?" Abu asked.

Manso took another sip from his calabash.

"Which is why you are illiterates," he said. "You hate anyone with an education. Your women desert you; the blame goes on someone's education. Friends, get a life!"

He took a long drink from the calabash.

"What would I do with your uneducated, drooped breasts and out-of-shape women? All they ever seem to want is to bear children and prepare food for fools like you."

"Hi, Education-man, PISS OFF," a voice shouted.

"Go back to Freetown if you want to see your thirty-first birthday," another voice intoned.

Abu raised an arm.

"Let him speak," he said turning to his friend. "If this is the way you feel, why do you want to be a member of our society?"

His friend sighed. The society did nothing for the community. With his education and the society's power behind him, they could improve Lunsar, even the Chiefdom. Coming to think about it, it was his heritage.

This made Abu laugh. He only wanted to use the society to further his own ends, he said. What he proposed was not possible.

"Who says?" He asked. "Water could be piped to the community or several new wells dug. Schools could be built; small businesses set up."

He watched their gaping faces.

"Of cause, these would further my own ends, but they will improve the lives of the people too,"

"Nothing but dream," Abu said.

"Exactly," he replied. "With non-progressives and stay-at-homers, like you, running things. You can choke on your society; see if I care."

He drained his calabash then stormed from the bar accompanied by a noisy send off.

During the rest of that day and most of the next, he stayed at home and fumed. Six o'clock that evening found him ensconced in a vantage point along the river his loaded weapon at his feet as were four large eels on the rapidly cooling earth. He happily cast his line for the umpteenth time and watched as the floater bobbed away. By eight, when the sky turned ink-black, one dozen of the beauties would be by his side, he thought.

He withdrew the line and examined the hook: It still had the bait. He recast. Watching the line sink into the water, he laughed aloud. He had been very rude in the palm wine bar and his friends were right: He came back intending to use his one-time friends but they saw through him. In the morning, he would apologize, especially to Abu.

The line suddenly jerked; he reeled it in to find the bait gone. He reached into the Ovaltine can for another then flung the line into the water.

'Wham,' an idea sent his heart racing.

"Nah," he said shaking his head. "That is not possible. God, can it be?"

There was another pull on the line, and it began paying itself out. He allowed his adversary free movement as it swam to midstream. He was reeling it in when twigs went, 'Sna-a-ap, crac-k-le,' behind him.

With bated breath, he turned to peer into the darkness.

The sounds crackled nearer still; a warm stream of sweat flowed down his cheek and neck even as icy fingers massaged his spine. He grabbed for his shotgun his heart pounded like a motor's engine.

The footsteps were now distinct each foreshadowing imminent disaster. Twenty yards away, two beady orbs reflected the glare from his hat lamp. Their owner swaggered into the pool of light with a gaping, salivating mouth. Its initial attack forced him backward putting him at the river's edge almost toppling him into the water.

He steadied himself and hoping the bullets worked brought the gun to his shoulder and took aim. The first shot went into the animal's left-back limb and sent him on all fours blood rushing from it. The next two tore into the right-front almost dismembering it.

Resisting the hypnotic pull of the beast's gaze and against the witchdoctor's orders, he put two more bullets into its torso.

The leathery skin split exposing pinkish flesh which made him wince. Blood gushed from the wounds; it made the animal stumble and thrash about as it endeavored to get to its foe.

He watched its struggles for a while then lowered his weapon and walked to his remaining blood-splattered equipment.

"If you are not human, why attack me while standing on your hind legs?" He asked putting his things together.

He turned but could just make out the behind of the animal, tail swishing from side to side, staggering into the bushes.

He rebuked himself for the numerous injuries he'd caused the animal on purpose; this prevented him from sleeping well that night. If the creature died, and it turned out to be human, he would have all hell to pay. He awakened his Dad in the early hours of the morning: Their discussion went on until well after two-thirty; at its end, he slept like a drunkard. He was aroused five hours later by loud banging's on the front door of the hut and cries of, "Manso-daddy, wake up. Come and see what is on the path leading up to your hut."

A group of women walking along a path, running from Morlai's house, on their way to their farms came upon a sight that had sent them charging back to the hut.

Their sleepy relatives ran with them to the sight of the problem: From a distance, they saw a being whose upper half was that of a person. It lay on its stomach—head toward the hut arms splayed out—blood everywhere. Getting nearer, they saw that the lower portion wasn't human but that of a crocodile.

With the females' help, they flipped over the body. What was exposed had the women wailing, disturbing the morning's calm. Some dropped to and rolled about on the ground. Others, shouting, tore at their head wraps then their hairs while they stamped their feet on the earth.

"Allah, be merciful," Morlai cried, clutching at his chest. He crashed to the ground eyes opaque, froth gushing from his mouth.

His son handed his unconscious form to other relatives then knelt by the creature.

Tears, unabashedly, poured down his face, and huge heartbreaking sobs wracked his frame: He was looking down on the face of his one-time best friend, Abu.

# Maligned

Black almond eyes surveyed the lithe figure sashaying toward the steps leading up to the hut. Salamatu marveled at the grace of her visitor's gait and the ease with which she balanced a container of sun-dried clothes on her head. She sighed as her visitor, Mearta, drew closer. Her eyes searched her face to discern her thoughts: Hadn't she noticed the commotion in the village? Why was she so calm? Was she thinking that the other housewives had started their evening meals late, again, and their children were adding to the general excitement and confusion?

She suppressed a sigh and wiped her face and sweat soaked armpits; her friend stood in front of her. She knew she would be anxious to see her offspring who she had been away from for the best part of the day.

"Good day." Mearta's greeting startled her. "What is the matter?"

She asked. "Did the she-devil make trouble again, today?"

The visitor's face showed a touch of concern and anxiety for the very first time.

"She didn't," Salamatu answered wiping her face again. "We slept for a while. When I woke up, she was gone."

She let out a low moan; Mearta had leaned against the wall by her side.

"Gone? And you sit here?" The latter asked. "Why aren't you searching for her?"

She moved from the wall and raced toward some clumps of grass calling, "Cumba? Cumba?" as she searched.

Salamatu wondered if she'd done the right thing by sitting on her doorsteps. Shouldn't she be out searching for the young girl? The consensus of the village, however, was that she stayed home.

"What will my husband say?" Mearta's voice reached her. "He told me to take the chile with me to the river; I refused. 'Salamatu will baby-sit the chile'," I said. "Now, she's missing. Agh Gawon (God), where is she?"

Salamatu winced. She was comforted when she heard a woman, who was by Mearta's side, say that the men would find the child. She couldn't have traveled far: She was just a year old. This said, she took the distraught mother's arm and walked her to her hut.

Word of the missing child got to the men before they left their farms for home.

Salamatu learned from her spouse, Kinney, that the body of the child had been found floating in a pond. When they came upon it, it seemed a simple case of a baby drowning. On it being retrieved, however, some of the younger men vomited while the youngest fainted: The neck of the child was broken and had teeth marks imprinted on it; large and deep, blood-clogged-claw marks scarred the torso. Where the heart should have been was a garish wound. The eyes and the flesh covering the face were absent.

Next evening, at a gathering of the villagers, the Chief wondered what could have caused such destruction.

Kinney suggested a leopard, a tiger or some other wild beast.

"No way," the Chief said. "Those animals will eat the feet and up. They won't take out the heart, eyes, and flesh from the face. Something else happened here."

"Easy now, Chief," Kinney said above the mutterings of the village women. "We don't want to alarm the women. You know—"

"Mercy Gawon, have mercy. Have mercy and save our children," drowned out his words.

The lament lasted for about twenty minutes then died down. In the ensuing silence, frightened eyes anxiously searched for and became relieved at the sight of their offspring's familiar faces then returned to the business at hand.

Their deeply held fears had been awakened. Seha, Salamatu's senior mate, voiced all of these with a simple whisper: It started in the ear of her best friend then reverberated around the village and, within a few minutes, was thundering beyond the village limits to echo among its hilly surroundings. Soon, females in Mattru-Jung, and those in villages bordering it, were searching for and herding their protesting youngsters into the comforts of their cozy huts.

To calm their fears, their husbands left for the forests instead of their farms two days later. They returned, after a few days and nights, with a leopard weighing around three hundred pounds and measuring some eight feet in length.

The quiet of that evening was shattered by boisterous singing and dancing around glowing bonfires.

Salamatu was conspicuous by her absence at these festivities. She couldn't understand how the memory of the imprints of the saber-like teeth on the mutilated child's tender neck could be replaced so soon by laughter and joy induced by huge amounts of palm wine and omole'(Gin).

Sitting quietly in her hut and slapping at the mosquitoes biting and buzzing in her ears, she thought of the events that had transpired since she'd married Kinney. It had been a troubling year, some would say a cruel one: Seha taunted her because she hadn't conceived within the first nine months; she tried getting their husband to send her back to her parents; these efforts failed. Her latest and most damning was about the missing girl and could cause her all sorts of problems, yet.

The situation grew worse over the following days; friends—Yahbom, her closest, excepted—who usually left their sobbing offspring in her care did not show up.

On the third day of her purgatory, Yahbom left her screaming boy, as usual, on her way to the market. She returned some hours later to pandemonium in the village: Her little boy was missing.

The sly and barbed whispers continued their roughish rounds. They gained momentum as the grayness of dusk overwhelmed the daylight hours and the boy stayed missing.

Seha called the boy's mother a fool, a simpleton. Why did she have to kowtow to someone without a child; someone so much younger that herself, a complete stranger? Couldn't she have left the child with a more experienced and discerning mother?

The women of the villages applauded these sentiments. They agreed that Mearta's girl and Yahbom's boy were sacrifices to Salamatu's Krifee, or devil. They wondered why it was now, after more than a year of trying for a child, and failing, their children were going missing. Such things had never happened in their villages before.

They prevailed on their spouses to search for the missing boy that very evening.

The men returned in the morning with the body which they found up in the fork of a sour-sop tree. The skull was cracked open and the brain missing. The body and face were masses of exposed muscles and clotted blood vessels.

In the days that followed, mothers would not let their

offspring out of their sights nor let them play outside even though they became nuisances in their boiling huts. A few were relieved when Seha prohibited them from associating with her mate: Most had all ready decided to do this without her say so.

Even Yahbom complied this time around: She couldn't stand being kicked out of the elite Bundo Society.

At the Society's head-quarts, the mutilations were debated, vehemently, for several days and nights. Some wondered how a woman who hoped to have children of her own could do such dreadful things to the children of others. They damned Kinney for marrying out of the Mende Tribe hence putting their children in danger.

Yahbom argued there was no proof that Salamatu was the perpetrator of these gruesome acts. She opined that clearer evidences were needed before her friend could be condemned.

The consensus was that Salamatu could stay in the village. Should children continue to die, however, within the next few days and weeks, the witch and her Krifee would be dealt with.

Meanwhile, mothers snatched their young ones away when these innocents continued to hug Aunty 'Salay' at the village center. On meeting her on isolated paths, eyes were averted and loud prayers offered to Gawon in heaven. Often, insults would precede long streams of snuff-stained spittle into her face.

"Woman who Gawon curse," her mate would shout across the fence separating their backyards, "Why won' you leave our chilren alone? If you Krifee call for chile-sacrifice, give him one of you own. However, Kinney get sense: He won' sleep with a witch, huh?"

The subject of these attacks would cry for hours. She pinned for the presence of Kinney in her hut. If only he came and stayed his usual month, everything would be fine. She received word that he would sleep with her only when she proved her non-involvement in the business of the mutilated children.

She prayed to Masala, her minor Krifee for his return: It failed. She brought out a satin-lined, white, wicker basket that contained her major Krifee, Ansari, and petitioned its help. Kinney still stayed away.

One week later, a neighbor's child went missing. Word went out, started by Seha, that the child had been playing in her mate's front yard. Vehement denials from the latter couldn't prevent her front door from coming down in a violent attack. Half-way through a severe beating she was rescued by the Chief's wife and Yahbom.

Later that afternoon, the child reappeared strapped to the back of an older sister: They had been down at the river playing.

Even when Salamatu sent him word about the hurt to her person and the damage to his property, Kinney didn't show. She left Mattru-Jung for Makeni the very next day without informing him.

She returned three weeks later accompanied by a young woman—of about fifteen—who had a baby tied to her back.

Several of the village women, temporarily struck dumb by their presence, followed them to her hut.

"So you come back, witch?" Her antagonist intoned from her front yard on hearing the commotion outside her mate's hut. "From which mother you steal that chile?"

Her mate silently walked into her hut from where she watched mothers who avoided her hut for weeks, when she alone occupied it, marched by taking furtive peeks through the hut's front windows and door.

The situation festered until early the next afternoon. The young girl, Salamatu's niece, came out and sped in the direction of Yahbom's hut.

Two minutes, three, flew bye then the owner emerged followed by the girl. They sprinted the twenty yards to Salamatu's hut.

Four hours—time when all activities in the village ceased—she spent in there. Time in which the citizens formed animated groups from which buzzing sounds emanated. They waited, as comfortably as the glaring sun and its choking heat could allow, for their un-chosen representative to reappear.

"What is the baby like?" Someone asked when she emerged.

"Hmm, beautiful," she answered. "Brown skinned and her hair is curly."

An angry murmur followed a minute's silence. Jockeying for position started around her.

"Is that all we hear from you?" A voice asked. "You stay in there for four hours and all you tell us is the color of the baby's skin and hair. Damn you, Yahbom, we want some more."

"Why bring the baby to this village?" Seha asked.

Yahbom realized they were becoming restive. Pushing back at their perspiring bodies she ordered them out of her way. If they wanted answers, they should go into the hut, themselves, and get them.

"Why bring the chile to this village?" Seha's voice insisted above the rising noise.

Yahbom brushed an offending hand from her buba (blouse).

"To show she cannot hurt a helpless child," she said. "She loves children. She is dying to have one of her own."

Loud sniggers accompanied her words.

"Who kill your son and Mearta's daughter?" Seha asked as she cleared a path for her.

Yahbom allowed her to take her arm as they walked through the crowd.

"With the child in her hut," she said, "She hope Gawon will

take pity and make her pregnant: That is if Kinney will sleep with her."

Laughter reverberated along the rolling, tree-covered hills that surrounded the village. Some were still holding unto their sides when Salamatu, carrying the baby, came out.

The laughter died instantly. And, as the village women watched, from concealed nooks and crannies, Salamatu and her niece, sitting on a mat, sang lullabies to the silent infant and crocheted baby things in front of her hut.

At one o'clock, the young girl went into the hut and returned with a basket balanced on her head. She stooped, picked up the baby, kissed it, laid it back on the mat, then left.

The aunt continued crocheting for another hour then hurried into the hut. No sooner had she done so than weird, growling sounds came from the bushes in front of the sleeping form.

She rushed to a front window to see a leopard's sharp claws rip into the baby's clothing and its gaping mouth engulf the tiny, curly head. Then, with powerful neck muscles, the baby was vigorously shaken then tossed into the air. A few more of these followed during which its arms fell off.

Salamatu had seen enough: She ran to a box in her bedroom from which she took a blanket with cowry shells and pieces of written-on paper sewn along its edges. She dashed outdoors and, ignoring the crowd that had gathered, threw it over the snarling, rampaging beast and the child. The animal shuddered and with the infant between its teeth bounded into the nearby bushes chased by Salamatu with the severed arms in hand.

The crowd of women, braying at their mouths, went after them with hastily acquired sticks and other available weapons.

The chase went on for more than ten miles with pieces of the blanket left behind on branches and the thorns of plants. It finally ended at an unnerving sight: A human form—feet exposed by the torn blanket—lay under the sour-sop tree from which Yahbom's mutilated boy had been retrieved.

Breathless but determined, Salamatu whisked one of the blanket's tattered ends off the prone forms. There were loud gasps and groans from the women.

"Mama? Mama?" The voice of a young child cried as he rushed forward to kneel by the still forms. "What did she do to you, Mama?"

He bent over the body of a woman who lay on top of that of the baby's. Her head was on its face and her arms wrapped around its tiny form.

The woman's body shuddered, twice, her breathing became labored then she laid still.

Salamatu with Yahbom's help flipped the body over.

The young child screamed, again, then crashed to the damp forest floor: He was Seha's son. His mother's face was smeared with a clay colored substance as were her exposed fang-like incisors. Her hands resembled those of a leopard with paws and long, sharp claws.

On examination of the remains of the battered child, they discovered it had become sticky under the scorching sun: It was a facsimile made with tar and smeared with clay colored paint.

# The Secular Ghost

Resplendent in white-naval uniform Ifayomi preened himself and occasionally saluted the dancers surrounding his lantern. He stood on the deck of a candle-lit ship in an Islam-oriented festival. Though not a Moslem, he had contributed enough money and time, to the group, 'ENDEAVOR' to get him his exulted position.

"You look every bit a Naval-officer," the Second-mate said eying the gold-colored buttons, epaulettes, and peaked cap on the First-mate's head.

That officer smiled though he seemed engaged, his eyes wandering over the crowd taking in the varying shapes and sizes of the bobbing hand-held lanterns.

He searched for no one in particular but admired the colorful costumes of the float's supporting groups. Finally, he saw a tall elegantly poised person who danced at the fringe of one of the groups.

"Doesn't she look ethereal in that white dress?" He asked, pointing her out to the Second-mate. "Why does it go to her shoes? I would like to see her legs."

His companion laughed.

"Don't know the answer to that," he said. "She is beautiful but she looks somewhat another-worldly to me. Why is she in a white dress? Fancy your chances with her?"

What does he mean by, 'another-worldly?' He thought. Of course, he fancied his chances but more importantly, how was he to get her on the float? His heart did an acrobatic flip-flop when she looked up and their eyes met. The look in hers made him want to jump off the float and dance by her side. Doing so, he realized, could keep him off the float for good.

The gyrating bodies that concealed her from him as they went down Kissy Road irritated him; he searched more fervently for the object of his fantasy. Something said he shouldn't be obsessed with a person he'd seen, for the first time, only thirty minutes earlier. He was not one to allow such a little problem to worry him. Maybe, he thought, if he invited her on board, when next he saw her, the pounding in his heart would cease and he could continue carrying out his duties onboard the float.

He got his Captain's permission for her to come onboard and started a more earnest search even leaning over the side of the float to see if she was around.

"Did she move to another group to dance with?" He asked himself.

"Psst."

Everyone seemed busy on board the ship.

"Psst."

He looked down at the dancers and, to his left, there she was smiling up at him. His heart raced at the radiance of her moonlit face. He gestured toward the steps leading up to the float.

She mouthed something that he could not hear above the singing and the noise of iron-wheels on an asphalt road.

He pointed at the steps leading up to the float and waited as she maneuvered through the bodies blocking the gangplank to the float. If he had thought her beautiful, from a distance, he knew that was an understatement. Standing close by, he studied her face: It was oval with a cherubic smile and her eyes were surrounded by delicate wrinkles giving it an air of sophistication and self-assurance instead of making it look old and tired.

He loathed taking his eyes off her but had to wave and occasionally raise his cap in acknowledgment of the words of praise being heaped on the float. He returned to her when the Captain invited Eva—which he knew by then—to stand by his side.

She said the First-mate invited her onboard and she didn't want to wreck his evening deepening the glow on that individual's face.

"How I envy you," the Captain said as he walked away leaving behind an ecstatic First-mate who had his arm around her by then.

As they made their way along Pademba Road, a mile-and-a-half down which the judging of the floats occurred the group's dancing became more frenzied. At the Secretariat Building, next to the centuries-old Cotton Tree—both splendidly lit for the occasion—on Siaka Stevens Street sat the excited and colorfully attired judges and important persons of the city.

"This is the part I hate," He whispered in her ear. "Why are all these (so called) dignitaries sitting around?"

"They lend dignity to the occasion," she said. "With the President and Mayor here, it gives the occasion respectability and color. Don't you just love our Mayor's ceremonial robs?" She added giving his fingers a squeeze.

"I just love gazing at you," he replied smiling. "You are far more pleasing to my eyes than fifty of those buffoons."

"Aw, go on," she whispered in his ear her face broking into a shy smile. "You do know how to make a girl feel wanted. I bet you say this to every woman you meet, Huh?" She freed one of her hands.

Very delicate hands, he thought: But why are they so cold? He began massaging the one he still held while he gazed into her face.

Her eyes were deep pools of dense fluids with something in them that caused him some unease. He entertained these feelings for all of two seconds then banished them from his mind, forever: He could cope with whatever occurred in the future.

It was fun, fun and laughter the rest of that early morning after the judging of the floats—they didn't win a prize. When not dancing or holding hands, at the Coconut Club, they sipped whiskies-on-ice and glasses of Bloody Marys respectively and he whispered sweet-nothings in her ears.

Three o'clock came and as he cooed more endearments to her, the hand he'd been stroking went limp. Her face had turned pale and was filled with fear. Turning around, in his chair, he saw that she stared at a party of six who had entered and stood about four tables from theirs and were staring in their direction.

"Is there something I can do?" He asked. "Those people are being rude: They are asking for trouble."

Her fingers gave his a slight squeeze.

"If they annoy you," he continued, "I can go up and talk to them."

Looking alarmed, she thanked him.

"That won't be necessary but I think we must leave at ones." She removed her hand from his and groped for her purse on the floor her eyes still on the group.

Something had gone terribly wrong here, he thought. Who were these people? Why would their presence cause so much consternation in her? If he were man enough, he would walk up and demand an explanation.

"Can we live, now?" Her hands relentlessly rubbed her

shoulders as she refused the offer of a new drink. "Don't think it's you," she said seeing the hurt in his eyes. "I had a wonderful time before that group arrived. Now, I'd be happy to leave."

She took his hands sensing the confusion in him.

"One of those individuals was my lover some years back," she said. "I dumped him two years ago. I bet he is wondering if it is I. Can we leave now, please?" She pleaded in a whisper. "I'll hate him to come up and ask questions."

"You dumped him two years ago; he seemed to have got over it, now. Why would he ask questions today?"

"That is another story." She said. "If we're together over the next few months, you will get to hear about it."

She collected her purse from the table and rose.

He called for the check, paid it off and led the way outside.

It was raining out there; she became restive and agitated when they were unable to flag down a taxi at once. She angrily walked to the junction of Wallace Johnson and Pultney Streets practically dragging him behind her under the rain.

"What part of Kissy Road?" The cab driver asked when they finally flagged one down and were traveling east on Kissy Street.

She said at the top end of the Road: You know the roundabout at the 'GUN' monument.

Her words had Ifayomi sitting bolt upright: When he'd first seen her, she had been by the Kissy Road cemetery. He thought he knew every woman who lived around that area. She might have moved to the vicinity only recently and since he had been busy—constructing the float—he did not get to know her.

"It's on occasions like these with so many people out on the streets," the Cabby said breaking the deafening silence in the vehicle, "that one should be careful."

Leaning on the back of his seat she said that it was no special night: Just another old night: There was nothing for one to worry about.

The Cabby laughed happily and honked his horn.

"Old folks say there would be ghosts about behaving like normal people on such nights," he said.

"There are no ghosts," Ifayomi said uncoiling like a spring and nearly hitting the back of the Front-passenger's headrest. "You Cabbies are all the same, out to spread rumors and make people afraid. There are no ghosts."

Eva smiled and took his hand,

"Are you sure?" She asked. "You mustn't think they don't exist because you've not met one. I haven't met one myself, but I believe in them."

Ifayomi settled back in his seat.

"Woman, I will believe in that nonsense if and when I meet one."

The Cabby laughed. He did not believe in them, either. However, just in case they did exist, he did not pick up weird-looking folks, traveling alone, on nights like this one: Many Cabbies had done so to discover they picked up something they didn't bargain for.

"You lose customers that way," Ifayomi said.

"Oh, brother," she joined the discussion. "There would be no trouble if you picked them up only as fares. Nefarious thoughts in some Cabbies' minds lead to the problems."

Ifayomi's eyes became wide open.

"The reason why I picked you up," he said into her ear. "And, what was that all about in the club? Are you hiding something from me?"

If she had something to hide, would she drink four Bloody Maries?

He returned to looking out of the window wondering why he

was so jumpy: He was a trained scientist; he shouldn't allow the words of the Cabby to bother him.

All fell quiet at the front of the cab after this outburst. At the back, the two silently fought over the possibility of kissing; Eva not allowing Ifayomi how hard he tried. At their destination, they alighted to stand on the round about as the Cabby drove away.

"Where do you live?" He asked taking her hand.

She did not reply for a while. She then said a little way down the road.

He wondered why they did not stop in front of her house. However, it did not prevent him from putting an arm around her waist.

She hummed, pleasantly, as they walked down the road her arm by now encircling his waist.

They came to a huge white-painted house standing in front of a cemetery's gate.

"She lives at Lady Smith's," he said Soto Voce.

"Huh?"

He said he was sorry; he'd been talking to himself.

"Worse fool me for having all those wild thoughts about her. I should be ashamed of myself." He said this to himself but received a gentle squeeze on his fingers and a question about his health.

Of cause, he felt fine; he now knew where she lived and with whom. He was not going to tell her that, though. He was so happy that at the gate leading into the yard, on which the house stood, he could not understand why she barred him from going in with her. Why shouldn't he? He asked. Didn't she enjoy their evening together? He could not go into the house but there was nothing wrong with him coming into the yard with her.

She asked why she should do that.

So they could do something they hadn't done all evening; embrace and kiss a little.

"No!" She flared. "You pressured me while we were in the taxi; I'm not that type of person. We only just met, today; hold your kisses for later."

They had a good time together; that warranted a good-bye kiss.

She was sorry he would not be getting one from her. She needed to know a bit more about a guy for that to happen.

"Good-bye." She rushed into the yard, slammed the gate in his face then ran a bolt.

He cursed and kicked at the gate. Why had he spent all his money and time on her? He raved. What was going on? Angry, frustrated and suspicious he walked away. At an adjacent building, he hid behind a stack of cement building-blocks at its front.

He was rewarded after half-an-hour's wait:

The gate to the White-house flew open and she ran onto the curb. She looked both ways along Kissy Road then crossed over to the cemetery. At its gate, she surveyed her surroundings. Seeing nothing alarming, she gracefully moved into the graveyard.

Ifayomi broke into hot flushes as he watched. He felt clammy fingers run the length of his spine. He wondered what business she had in a cemetery that early in the morning.

Getting to his feet he raced across the road to stand at the cemetery's gate. He could just make out her form through the veil of mist.

As she moved slowly among the gravestones, her feet seemed to glide over the ground.

He entered the cemetery on noiseless feet moving from one built-up grave to another. He watched her move toward the door of a grass-covered, dilapidated-stone vault with a facsimile of a female human head in front.

She stopped, looked searchingly around then waited a few minutes.

Ifayomi—in his haste to get closer to where she stood—had tripped over an earth-packed grave in the dark. He sat on the ground wondering what he had gotten himself into not daring to move. Three minutes later, he rose on his knees and looked over a granite headstone in front of him.

She still stood before the vault staring in his direction. Her lovely face now a taunting, malicious mask had barred her rotted gums in an unwholesome grin. The flesh on her face slid down in waves of a waxy, gooey mess which left an exposed skull with scraggy hairs on top. With wizened and scrawny fingers, she plucked her eyes from their sockets, gave an unholy scream then passed through the unopened door into the vault.

"Heaven help me," he cried in his hiding place. Thirty years after his fifth birthday, he wetted and shitted on his pants as a constricting pain engulfed his frame. With froth gushing out of his mouth and nostrils, he fell down on his face: This time in a dead faint.

# Wanton Feelings

The clacking keys blurred as I typed a letter at my desk.

"I will do away with it?" I heard myself say, angrily.

I, Mandy, had astonished my doctor with those very words on my second visit with him. He'd asked for my reasons for wanting to do what I'd suggested. Sweat poured from my body that would later stain my white-cotton blouse, at the armpits, leaving glistering islands of moisture on both sides of my breasts.

"I am just not ready for a child," I explained. "I have a year and a bit in this god-forsaken place then I'll be bound for London."

I rose from the table, took a deep breath and asked if the examination was over.

"It is," the Medic said. "An abortion isn't a good idea; you are at the earlier stages of the pregnancy and may want to keep it as you get used to it."

"Not a chance of that happening, Doc," I said grimacing. "Not when my fiancé' waits for me in Birmingham. I can see the revulsion in his face when he finds out I became pregnant by another man."

He'll likely murder me when he discovers the child is black, she thought.

"No, it's got to be my way. I cannot risk him finding out."

I vigorously shook my head; I had to forget that particular visit. Taking a deep breath, I made some corrections to the document in front of me and took it in to my superior.

"What is the matter, Mandy?" The latter asked setting eyes on me. "You look about to collapse; hope I haven't been overworking you?"

I said no but I would like to go home for the rest of the day, though. I would be at work early the next morning.

Driving along Oxford Street in my white Ford Consul (about three hours later) I thought back to my time in the town. I had turned twenty-one a week before I made the first visit to the Medic. He informed me I was a strong and healthy individual but for malaria and the heat. The former was common to every expatriate living in the country he told me and not even the Natives could better the heat. I felt I'd weathered the ravages of the tropics well; maybe, the heat was finally getting to me. It affected some people that way I'd been told.

I'd arrived in front of my home—up in the Spur Loop Hills—without realizing it. I should pay more attention to what I did I thought as I entered the house. I poured a large glass of orange juice, from the refrigerator, and drank it with two aspirins. Within half an hour, I was in slumber-land to awaken, in the late evening, to ingest a croissant and a glass of milk before crashing back into bed.

The walls of the bedroom were pulsating, like an agitated heart, when I woke up to what I thought was the next morning. I staggered toward the restroom that hovered about a mile away on wobbly legs. I had better hurry to it, I thought: Not wanting to mess my nicely Mansion-polished floor with vomit.

I rinsed out my mouth then returned to the bedroom. By its wall clock I saw that I'd slept through the next morning. I dialed my work place and gave the reason for my absence. Getting on to my physician, on the phone, I explained the way I felt and said I'd slept through nearly a whole day. Medications were prescribed for the vomiting and he advised me to lie in bed for a few days.

During this time in bed, I thought about my stay in Freetown. As I said earlier, I had been in the country for about a year and it had been terrible to me. I'd arrived full of ideas about how to enjoy my two-year stay. People, in England, who'd worked here before, told me life was one great ball: The problems being the heat and the mosquitoes.

I hated it the moment I stepped foot at the Queen Elizabeth Quay; life in the capital was quite pleasant and most of the people—especially the expatriates—were nice, but I loathed the citizens.

I thank God most of them lived in the East and Central parts of the town, with their dense population, shabby houses and congested roads. I lived up in Spur Loop Hills—in the West—where the place was less densely populated cooler and more like my home town—with flower gardens, parks and woods—in Britain.

It took me a day, on arriving at The Secretariat Building, my workplace, to decide that my black male co-workers were down right rude; they leered at one and stripped off ones clothing with their eyes. Their female counterparts stared with hatred at one as if one had intentions on their lascivious men to whom they seemed subservient and docile.

What offended me most, always making me want to puke, was that no matter what time of day, I could smell their musky aroma. Later, I learned that most bathed two to three times a day but due to the heat they perspired continuously. This did not lessen my aversion to their odor: Couldn't they use some perfume to mask it? I often asked.

I had painstakingly avoided dating or befriending any of them. Not that they hadn't tried dating me; during my first month, those who were self-assured, brazen enough, and were at per or higher, in the Service, to me, tried and were rudely rebuffed putting a damper to the enthusiasm of the others.

This situation prevailed well into my eighth month when weird things started happening. The first was a gentleman's handkerchief left in the top drawer of my desk. I was surprised because I always made sure these were locked, with keys, before going home.

The handkerchief was covered with spooky writings and stained with, what was determined to be, dried blood.

Expatriate colleagues who were in the country far longer than I had were upset. Such a display, they cautioned, could mean one of two things: Someone had it in for me and wanted to frighten me, or somebody was out to make me his love slave.

Couldn't happen to me I thought until I arrived at work one morning to find a parcel on my desk. I almost fainted on opening it to find a black-kid's horn around which was tied a red ribbon soaked with vile smelling oil and some more spooky writing in what I came to learn was Arabic.

Against my more knowledgeable workmates protestations, I picked up the horn to examine it: It fell onto my desk; I'd been pricked by some sharp object embedded in it.

I wouldn't let a thing like a pin prick bother me, friends who worried over the matter, were told. Later, I discovered, I'd fallen in love with one of my native co-workers, Sammy, a junior officer. Soon we were dating much to the frustration and chagrin of the other white expatriates.

My aversion to the Natives' noxious smells was gone. I grew to love taking long walks—along roads, gardens, and parks in my section of the town—with him our fingers intertwined. Two months into the relationship, after a cinema show and while we enjoyed ourselves at the Palm Beach Club, at Lumley Beach, things changed.

The new day was still in its infancy when I felt the juices flowing from my private parts: The sight of him dancing with some woman who had walked up to our table and marched him off to the dance floor, without my permission, enraged me. Seeing them grind their sexual parts together to a slow African beat added fuel to my angst. For the first time since arriving in Africa, I loathed someone because of her actions.

"What is wrong with me?" I asked fidgeting with a glass of untouched iced brandy and fighting the urge to rise and rush the dance floor to separate them. I however remained glued to the chair until the music ended, and he returned to the table.

"Did you two have to dance so closely?" I asked, as he settled into his seat. "Bet you thought you were riding her in bed, huh? We have been going together for all of two months and all you've done is kissed me like I'm your damn sister."

He gestured that I shut up.

The other patrons, mostly Natives, were becoming interested in our altercations.

I shouldn't let him talk to me that way I thought grabbing his hand and dragging him to the dance floor. With my groin grinding into his, I thrust my tongue into his mouth.

"Take me home; your home," I gasped my tongue working his mouth like a piston. "I'm hot for you; so hot, you'll have to take me right here, on this dance floor, if you don't."

He took me home that morning and the minute we entered his apartment, on Sanders Street in the West-end of the town, and while we leaned against the front door my hand flew to his crouch and unbuttoned his flap. Soon, his pair of trousers lay unbelted on the floor. I grabbed for his Y-fronts and tore it off, reached for his erect member and, with my mouth working his tongue, massaged it. I moaned as he played with my teats through my blouse.

"Damn you," I shouted, "take the stupid thing off."

Slowly, his hands moved downwards to reach under my skirt to finally rip off my soaking-wet lingerie. One finger made its way into my pussy and began massaging my clitoris, soon there were two. I let out prolonged sighs and several loud gasps; something deep within my brain violently pulsated its way down to my vagina: I screamed when it exploded within it and my body furiously banged against his as I came.

The master lifted my limp form into his bedroom and before I knew it, my clothes were lying on the floor and we were in bed. His tongue and fingers then began Lesson Two; things were done by them, on my breasts and pussy I had only imagined or read of in books. I learned that my ears had duties other than hearing and that my eyes were not only for seeing. His fingers played my body like a harpsichord; his expertise opened my eyes to the art of lovemaking; we did things my fiancé, back home, would blanch to think of let alone do. By the time I left for home, that evening, we had intercourse three glorious times. My body was tingling all over and I was in my own personal heaven.

Mine became an all-consuming passion; I was at his pad, every day, after work for weeks and many a time, left for work from there. I couldn't get enough of him even during working hours. I'd stroll over to where he labored and send covetous glances at his bent head. I'd be typing important documents which would be abandoned as I rushed to the restroom to release the raging and rampant feelings between my legs by fingering my pussy to an organism. My life became one big longing for him which got satiated, mostly in the evenings, when his erect member vibrated within my pulsating glory hole.

Months of our wanton, unabated lovemaking passed before

noticing that I easily got tired and was sick almost every other morning. We'd used condoms—excepting for the first three times—when making love so I couldn't be pregnant, I thought. You never knew with these Natives, my heart said: The reason I'd procured the condoms myself. What could have happened? I would die if I were pregnant; I hadn't bargained for that. No way, sister dear.

I'd paid my doctor that first visit and was told it was malaria and the heat. On my second visit, though, he'd tested for and found I was two months pregnant. I worried over whether Sammy would agree to an abortion for weeks. Would I be able to do away with the baby, if he insisted I kept it? Would I withstand the gossips of my workmates, if I did?

I smiled: My life was completely changed now; there were big decisions to be made about the pregnancy and my life from then on. Also, I couldn't go to bed with a white-man, ever again not even if my life depended on it; he just wouldn't satisfy my lust, wanton and aroused feelings.

Another three weeks flew by before Sammy was informed about the pregnancy. He seemed uninterested when I said I had something to tell him.

"Don't you want to know what the news is?" I asked.

"You'll tell me in your own good time," he replied.

I demurred for a while.

"Well, I saw my Medic about a month ago," I said finally. "He says I am about three months pregnant."

"He did?" He asked jumping up and rushing to my side. "Tell me some more, woman. How is my boy?"

"Too early for that, it could be a girl," I said. "I am thinking of having an abortion."

"What?" The word exploded out of him. "You'll do away with my boy? Are you crazy, woman? Don't I get any say in the matter?

I have waited for years, since I turned twenty-two, for some woman to tell me she is carrying my son and you tell me you want to do away with him? Lady, you need your head examined."

I grabbed him by the hands.

"My fiancé is in England, you know that. I hope to go back to him, soon. You had women before we met. How would you feel if your girl came back with a child not yours, the child of a white man?"

He shrugged. "I would hate it," he said, "probably kill her. I don't know about you going back to England, soon, though." He had a cunning look to his face. "You will stay here in Freetown and you'll have my son then do whatever you think is right for you."

"Of all the nerve, who is going to stop me?" I asked. "I came into this relationship with my eyes wide open; I can end it whenever I want."

"You would think so, huh?" he asked. "You are mine to do what with. You better stop talking nonsense about an abortion. You'll have the baby even if it kills you."

I didn't need his permission to do away with the pregnancy I told him. I was a grown woman whose body we were discussing. On Friday, I would see my gynecologist and ask that the pregnancy was terminated. I then stormed out of the apartment.

I brooded and couldn't sleep for several days after that. On the Wednesday, of the following week, I arrived at work to find a peace-offering from Sammy; in it were a bottle of Evening in Paris; a bouquet of red roses, and a beautifully worded card. I was pleasantly surprised; the first two were both favorites of mine and I just loved the words on the card: He sure knew how to get to where I lived, in several ways.

Moved by his thoughtfulness, I unconsciously splashed some of the perfume on my fingers and dabbed it behind my ears and on my arms over the next two days before going to work. It smelled heavenly and I thought of the sender who was conveniently not at work on those days.

What did he do at home, during that period? I couldn't wait to be in his arms. Rage coursed through my frame: I would kill him if he were with someone else, not when I carried his unborn child within me. Saturday, in the evening, saw me on my way, driving like someone demented, to his apartment.

He was at home walking around half naked in the flat.

"I knew you'd come," he said with that dimpled smile of his. "You can't live, without my member's rampage in your pussy, can you? And, above all, you carry my seed within you, now."

I said, "No. You are lucky I met you alone, though," I continued. "If I had met some woman here, both of you would have been dead by now."

I then fell on his partially naked skin and was soon in my special heaven.

Love for the being within me made my heart flutter and lurch as the days flew by. Soon, I found myself massaging my slightly bulging stomach every so often. I must be going crazy I thought: Only a few days ago, I was bent on destroying that fetus. Now, I had this growing feeling of love for the damned thing.

Did wearing Sammy's perfume make me change my mind or had he sensed my love, for the being, underneath all my protestations? I shivered: A feeling of maternal joy surged through me. There was nothing I wouldn't do to bring the new life—an extension of our love, I thought—into the world, now. I would kill so that my baby could be born.

If Sammy proposed, I would gladly marry him and reside in Freetown with all its problems for the rest of my life. If he didn't, I would return to Britain, have the child, and face the consequences. No one could make me do away with my child now; I would rather die than have an uncalled-for abortion.

# A Nagging Tongue

Judith's hands trembled as they clutched at her aching throat; her Physician's earlier diagnosis—her symptoms were those of a swollen tongue—prevented her from panicking. That information had been a relief: A small matter like a swollen tongue, she'd thought, shouldn't derail her life's only pleasure—haranguing her spouse, Frederick.

The nagging was worse, on this Wednesday morning, as they traveled to their small grocery store at Langley Park, Maryland. It got so nasty and violent that Frederick pulled on the steering wheel making the vehicle veer into the left lane missing a Ford Taurus by inches.

"Please honey," he said, "less nagging today. Well, less nagging until we get to the store or you'll involve me in an accident."

"I won't do that," she said. "What about your behavior at the store? Our customers snigger as you ogle Mrs. Anthony when she makes her daily visits. You just couldn't take your eyes off her; you practically undress and fondle her in your mind. You are a damned fornicator."

"Never ogled the woman," he said fighting with the Camry as

it strayed to the left, again. "I have too many customers to serve while you do nothing, but act superior, all day."

His mate's hands went out to brace her body against the dash.

"Damn it, man," she said. "Look the hell where you are going or let me drive."

Her hen pecked better half prevented the car from hitting a Mazda 626 that had cut into the space in front of them.

"Many times, we speak only briefly," he said as if nothing had happened. "Shouldn't I take her orders for spare-ribs and pounds of steak when she comes? Are you going to replace the money her absence would bring?"

"And that's the reason you almost chopped off the fingers of your left hand, some days ago, huh? You should do that for every customer that comes for meat."

She hit the dash board with her out stretched arms, again; Frederick had suddenly stopped and given the Mazda's driver a two-finger sign instead of listening to her.

Turning he said, "Funny you said that. The reason we have customers is I joke with the females and make them laugh. Things would go belly-up if it were left to you with your superior airs and turned-up nose."

"Rubbish, dear," she said shifting in her seat. "You chat up the female customers to prove you have a way with the opposite sex."

Frederick laughed heartily.

"What do you know?" He asked. "We are jealous. It's not that, my dear; I don't think I am too good to talk to them. They provide our wages."

She slowly turned to face him her hands still bracing her body against the dash. He should try being less offhanded with their male customers, then; show the world he had no hidden motive in chatting up only the females.

"Me? What hidden motives?" He asked. "Look, dear, stop

being a sourpuss and start buttering up our male patrons. You need to smile more: Men avoid the store because of your attitude."

What was he on about, she wanted to know.

He told her to look into a mirror; she would see why men avoided the store: She should try being more pleasant and laugh a bit more with the customers. Making a joke or two would have them returning for more. But knowing her, she would remain the bitter, domineering hag and pompous individual until the day she died.

The hands that went for his throat couldn't be escaped. Their force knocked his head against his side window and the vehicle swerved into the lane to their left forcing its traffic aside. He fought to stop the skid but almost side-swiped another vehicle only to stop when their car rammed into a Benz in front.

Its angry driver jumped out, surveyed the damage and beat a noisy tattoo on Frederick's window.

"Hey man, why the hell don't you watch how you're driving?" He asked. "Come out and see the damage you've done."

Frederick got out of his vehicle; the damage was not as bad as he'd thought. He told the owner that repairs to the vehicle could be carried out without the police coming in: He gave the irate driver his name and that of his Insurance Company, both addresses and telephone numbers. Each then made his way back to his car.

"Some spouse you are," Judith snapped the minute he stepped into his. "Why did you call me a virago to a stranger? I could strangle you. I wish he'd insisted you waited for the police."

He laughed. Wouldn't she just love to see him in a Jessop-Correctional-Institute uniform? He asked. The next fifteen minutes saw him being berated while they stewed in a traffic jam.

She was out of the vehicle, heading toward the store even

before it stopped completely. Her frantic search in her purse proved futile.

"Frederick?" She called her right foot beating a tattoo on the concrete sidewalk. "Hurry up and open the door: We've got customers waiting."

The rate of her foot striking the sidewalk increased as he continued searching for something in the vehicle's trunk.

She took two steps toward him.

"Didn't you hear me, Frederick," she shouted. "Come over this minute and open the door. Do you want our customers to wait all day?"

Continuing his search, he said if she was in such a hurry, she would come for the keys; it was senility that made her leave hers at home.

She controlled her anger even though she was bristling. Her opportunity for a pay-back came at around noon with the pace of the day's business nearing its peak and while Mrs. Anthony waited for her order.

Mrs. Dupreh—small, white haired, their oldest customer—came in and shuffled up to the Butchery section and asked for two pounds of lamb's meat for her dinner at the old people's home.

From her vantage point, at the front of the store, Judith watched her mate's preparations for the sale. She lost him, momentarily, when he moved behind a display unit that obscured the sink at the butcher's block. Checking out the customer before her, she handed the station to a subordinate then took off in the direction of the Butchery section.

She arrived about the time her spouse—knife in hand—delivered the first cut into the meat for the old lady.

"Hold it, buster," she blurted out racing up to them. "You have to wash your hands before cutting that meat."

Her spouse plunked the piece of meat on the scale.

"Wish this were your tongue," he said wiping his hands on his apron. He read two-and a half pounds off the scale then threw the meat on a piece of wrapping paper. "You didn't see me wash them," he said wrapping up the meat and looking at the old woman. "Mrs. Dupreh, here, did."

"He did, too," the old woman said without being asked. "Think I'll accept meat prepared by unwashed hands, Chile? I may be old but I am not senile."

She gave Judith a condescending stare.

"No one asked you old-withered face," the latter said. "Keep out of my affairs, you old hag."

Her words brought horror filled gasps from other customers. Only the one alluded to seemed momentarily unaffected then her face sagged.

"Mind your tongue, you struck up bitch," she said. "Your attitude will lose you customers." She turned and hobbled out of the store aided by Mrs. Anthony both leaving their cuts of meat on the counter.

Frederick whose eyes had gone stilt-like and whose hands were rolling and unrolling themselves into fists stood silently by.

"You had to be rude to her?" He asked finally. "I tell you woman you'll lose us the few customers we have. Can't you keep a civil tongue in your bloody mouth?"

She told him to shut up; if he'd washed his hands; they would not have lost Mrs. Dupreh's patronage. I hate when he has that faraway look in his eyes she thought as she turned on her heels to storm toward her checkout point: It means; he thinks. He doesn't do that often but when he does, he comes up with fanciful ways to deal with me.

She stopped, swiveled around and hurried to where he stood. She belted him in the mouth taking him unawares.

"You now have several reasons for retaliating," she said.

She walked away, her head held high, while her victim dabbed at his injured mouth with a wad of paper towels.

"No, dear," he said taking off after her, "it was your fault. You couldn't accept the truth: You couldn't believe; I washed my hands. You only retaliated for what happened this morning."

His spouse thought he had read her thoughts perfectly.

"Had nothing to do with this morning," she said aloud. "I didn't see you wash your hands. The old crow had no business in our discussion."

She stopped talking her face becoming a kaleidoscope of surprise and fear. She gulped down mouthfuls of air then continued,

"Her mind wanders." Her tongue had grown a lot lager, she thought, since she started her harangue. This was no reason for her to stop.

"She isth sthentild," she said the tongue obstructing the rhythm of her breathing; it pressed hard against her teeth and the roof of her mouth. It hurt so much that for a moment she thought of giving up her life's only pleasure. When she felt something tug at the bottom of her throat, she almost screamed.

"Do what I wanth," she determinedly continued on after controlling the offending organ. "If—"

Her hands flew to her throat: It was as if her tongue had become un-anchored.

Something wriggled up her throat, like a worm creeping out of a hole in the earth, causing spasms in its muscles. Three massive coughs wracked her body: At the third, a muscular organ shot out of her mouth to fall on the floor between them. It fluttered about in its pool of blood then laid still.

The gaping, awestruck customers rushed to the site.

Judith was speechless for once. She wished she had been more civil to Mrs. Dupreh who could easily be her grandmother. Also, she should stop beating on Frederick. Her tongue falling out was, maybe, retribution for being so discourteous to people over most of her life. If her tongue was ever fixed, she would try to be more civil to people, especially their customers, as Frederick had suggested.

"Get the Ambulance," she heard a female voice scream, belatedly.

Her spouse, who had observed the drama, in a trance, came to life. He hurried to the telephone, spoke into it then ambled over to the blood-splattered sink to painstakingly wash previously clean hands with copious amounts of water and soap. These were rinsed again and patiently wiped dry with a brand new roll of paper towels. The nails, of every finger, on both hands, were then examined, thoroughly.

Seemingly satisfied with the job he'd done, he walked to the wad of bloodied paper towels he'd used on his mouth, rolled into a ball and placed by the sink.

With it in his spotlessly clean hands, a smug smile on his face, he ambled over to the tongue, snatched it up then casually made his way to his Butcher's block.

Judith, and those customers still present, looked on as he chopped it into many small pieces with a cleaver the smug smile still on his face.

Blood drained from his spouse's face. Her mouth, wide open, was distorted in a soundless scream.

# War in the Making

"They think we are stupid and weak," Bureh said crumbling a letter he held into a ball and dashing it to the earthen floor in his hut. "Pay taxes on huts we built with our sweat, and the earth Allah gave us?"

He thought the Governor was mad.

Walking over, Alimmamy picked up the paper, smoothed it out, and joined Bureh in pacing the floor of the visitor's room. They then stopped to watch the moonlight, in the warm Yonibana evening, stream in through an open window.

Bureh knew he was in a bind: If he advised his people not to pay the tax, it would eventually lead to a war. Scores of young men had gone to early graves during such fights. This led to the preponderance of women in the Chiefdom. But, if they obeyed the order, they would forever be under the grabbing hands of the damned British.

"Sleep on the matter, Chief," Alimmamy's voice broke into his thoughts. "The order is indeed troubling, but you know the British; we don't want their anger on our people, at this time."

The Chief turned to face him.

"Don't you see?" He asked in a troubled voice. "This is a step in their taking over and directing our lives. Now, we have to pay a tax on our huts; next, they'll tell us when and what to plant in our farms. Then it will be when to make children and the number to make. Who do they think they are?"

"Our lords and masters," Alimmamy said. "They have the guns to make themselves so."

It's always their guns, thought Bureh looking away from him. A terrible time it is when even he is afraid to stand for the People's rights. When the white man came with his guns, such men as him became timid; they began behaving like women. He walked to a window and looked up at the twinkling stars.

"We should fight!" he said quietly. "Use their blood to nourish our soil: Throw them back to the coastlands from which they came."

His companion smiled.

"They are not the Kroos," he said. "They are good at making war and with their guns could wipe out our war boys."

The Chief pulled on his graying goatee.

"When have we been afraid to die?" He asked. "When have our men been so humbled that they refuse to fight for their rights?"

His subordinate realized that if they paid the tax without any resistance, the British would have the run of the land. Stupidly, he had assured Superintendent Thomas that there would be no trouble over the matter.

"If we pay up, Boss," he said his fingers crossed behind his back, "They will develop our roads and give us piped water. Even send our children to their schools."

"Leave me, now," the Chief ordered. He was troubled by his Senior Adviser's views; he seemed to be on the enemy's side. "The problem will be solved tomorrow in the evening."

To which effect, the drums beat early the next morning

announcing a meeting to be held, at the community's prayer ground, just before sundown that day. Bureh knew he would have only this opportunity to arouse his subjects against the tax. His 'Stool' was at stake: If he failed he would soon find himself, eventually, going to Freetown in chains.

Six p.m. came; the number of citizens at the grounds slowly increased: An air of festive gaiety pervaded the assembled people. The volume of the men's voices rose in mild banter, and the songs and laughter of the women—at the back—climbed to meet the gently rolling clouds that lined the evening sky.

Into their midst swept the Chief followed by his high officials. A hush fell on the assembly as they adjusted to the scene before them. Their rulers were in war paraphernalia—Ronkos to ward off bullets and arrows; head gears from the feathers of a Korkor bird, to dispel with evil spirits, and all the trappings that went with these.

It had been a while since the ruling class was seen in such finery: Not since the Kroos were driven into the River Rokel, some fifteen years back, had most witnessed such a sight.

The situation made the young men restive; they spoke excitedly among themselves. They had been too young to take part in that war and were certain that their growth into manhood and the higher echelons of power in the community had been impeded by this.

The older men with more wars behind them than they cared to remember shook graying heads, knowingly, and drew on white beards. They were wistful: They wished for youthfulness so they could wear war paints and prance about on study legs once more.

The Chief beckoned for silence. Waving the crumpled letter from the District Officer in his hand he said, "My people, for the past fifteen years, we have been peaceful, is it not so?"

"For too long," the young men shouted as they sat in front of the women.

"In that time," the Chief said clearing his throat, "we have watched the White man move from the coastlands claiming every thing in his path." He paused. "We didn't mind, seeing the lands he took belonged to others and were given to black men like ourselves who now think they are better than us."

The old men sitting at the front of the assembly shook their fists and walking sticks saying they should have kicked them all the way back to where they came from.

"True," The Chief said. "We didn't. We know who to blame for that."

With arms akimbo, and a mischievous smile on his face, he surveyed the staring faces. Every head was nodding.

He smiled. "Would anyone say I am a war monger if, for fifteen years, I watched my people being deprived of lands given to them by their forefathers? Would anyone call me a bigot if I say that since the White man came, from the coastlands, he has heaped nothing but shame on us, especially our men?"

"No," the assembly cried.

"If any thing, Chief," said a quivering young voice, "We say that at last, you talk like a man, and our chief."

He smiled: He had always been a man and their chief. Certain of his advisers had wanted him to give the British a chance; see what they would do. Everyone now knew what the British could do.

There was silence: Every eye was glued to his face; the time had come to make his play.

"Yes, we know what the White man could do: Steal our lands; murder our young men, and have their ways with our wives. These we have come to expect. Now, they have gone raving mad, crazy; they've ordered us to pay a 'Hut Tax.'"

Cutting into the silence that ensued, a young male voice from the back asked,

"Chief, what is Tax?"

"Yes," chimed an elder, "what is Tax, Chief? Huts we know about, but Tax—?"

The Chief signaled to Alimmamy who got up and explained it was a contribution levied on owners of huts and should be paid once a year in money or, its equivalent in produce.

"You mean; I pay money for my hut?" The surprised Chief Imam asked. "Why?"

"The hut I build with these hands?" The Chief's Head war-boy asked hands extended. "The one I build on land my father give me?"

Bureh said yes.

"If you refuse to pay, you'll be put in their jail until you do."

The Head war-boy laughed.

"Crazy fools," he said. "I will not pay and, with my boys, will be ready to fight, Chief."

He was silenced by the raised arm of the Chief: He wanted no talk of war he said the smile returning to his lips. Alimmamy was in favor of their paying up seeing they didn't stand a chance against the might of the British. He shut up: A missile from the back of the assembly had struck the Chief Adviser on the nose making it bleed.

"As for me," went on the Chief, "I refuse to pay. But I won't tell you what to do in the matter; you'll have the chance to decide and let the British know what you think of their tax, and what you'll do about it."

He sat down: His Chief Adviser, hand to his nose, had risen to speak.

"The Chief believes," he began, "that paying a 'Hut Tax' is bad: It isn't. In Freetown, house owners pay a tax and they are none the worse for it."

"That is true," The Chief said. "However, the British built their houses: The taxes they collect are used for building roads, schools, and for piping water. We have none of these things why should we pay any tax?"

"What happen to our taxes?" The Chief Imam asked. "How do we know it won't be used to develop Freetown at our expense?"

"I don't have—Alimmamy began but a barrage of missiles fell on him, and he quickly sat down. He had been outwitted by Bureh. The people were becoming restive and would do any thing in that mood.

The Chief rose and said they had seven days to reply to the directive. After that, the British threatened to send Tax Officials and armed Policemen to carry out the order.

A section head, Sheku, of the war boys advised that they refused to pay: Platoons of their war boys were being trained in the use of new weapons and they should be able to throw the white dogs off their lands. He was heard out by the Chief.

"The Elders decide when we fight," the latter said, "and on my advice. We must show hands and see if the People want to pay the 'Hut Tax.' If they vote no, we tell the British no; if they vote yes, we'll tell them the Tax would be collected when they paid for the lands they took from us and the produce and minerals they grab and send to their country for nothing."

The Senior Adviser asked what would happen when the British turned these down.

It would depend on them the Chief said; since they came, they had preached one-man-one-vote. They had to listen when the People voted not to pay the 'Hut Tax.' If force was used, it would be going against the People's will.

"Then, I'll gladly advice that we fight."

A tumultuous cheer arose from the assembly: They recognized the wisdom of their Chief.

"Let us show our hands," the men sang. Let us show our hands."

The question was put; and, as the voices of their women and children sang in the background, and the setting sun caressed the hills in the distant horizon, with a show of hands, the men voted not to pay the 'Hut Tax.'

"The People have spoken," The Chief said. He then empowered Alimmamy with sending the People's reply—which he would dictate—to the District Officer's directive.

The D.O. fumed on receiving the Chief's reply. He ordered his Chief of Police—Superintendent Thomas—to visit the Chiefdom.

The policeman doubted if the problem could be solved by his presence in the Chiefdom. He knew that arms and their munitions had been bought by the Chief in the event of a war. He'd warned the D.O. but he wouldn't listen: No savage black-man had the gumption to buy, nor the intelligence to operate such sophisticated weapons in his eyes.

Thomas reluctantly arrived at the Chief's courtyard. It seemed he was expected: Everyone, but for the Senior Adviser and the Witchdoctor, wore his war paraphernalia and carried weapons. He salaamed to the Chief, nodded to his officials then sat on a stool, lower than, and a few places to the left of the Chief's. He waited.

Bureh took his pipe from his mouth. With whisk beating at the flies he said, "We greet you in peace. We hope your presence here won't be a waste of everyone's time."

The pipe was handed to a war boy behind his stool.

Thomas had permission to speak.

"Greetings from the D.O., Chief," he said, "He hopes I find you well?"

Bureh smiled. He liked Thomas. He realized the inquiry about his health was Thomas' but custom demanded that he attributed it to his superior.

"What news do you bring us?" he asked.

The Superintendent took a deep breath.

"The D.O.," he said, "received your reply to the payment of the 'Hut Tax.' He's worried about its tone."

"What do you mean, by its tone?" He asked.

Alimmamy sitting immediately to his right leaned toward him and whispered in his ear.

He nodded then said, "What about its contents?"

Thomas said the D.O. understood the contents. He felt, however, the tone was too aggressive and harsh. His refusal to collect the 'Hut Tax' would cause the Sub-Chiefs to follow in his footsteps.

"Soon, there would be war on both your hands."

The Chief had listened with his eyes closed. He opened them and said: "What war? We said nothing about a war. You teach us about your democracy; we used it. The People voted not to pay the tax."

He waited for Thomas to speak. He didn't.

"You meant the vote to be used against the Chiefs and their elders; when it's turned on you, you speak of war. Tell the D.O., if he wants one, he'll find us able opponents."

Thomas realized the situation was slipping out of his hands.

"He doesn't want war," he said. "We hear of you buying rifles and munitions from the Arabs. We think you have enough now to outfit twenty platoons of your war-boys. The D.O. thinks this is an excuse for you to fight a war."

"I wish we had those rifles and their munitions," he said. "You are welcome to search my Chiefdom at anytime. If you find rifles, other than our Shakabullahs, seize them and imprison their owners."

The Policeman grinned.

"We know they are not in your possession as yet," he said. "We will be watching the Chiefdom closely. When they are brought here, you'll be in chains on your way to Freetown."

The Chief shrugged his shoulders.

"What the British do with their time," he said, "is none of our business. We will not pay the 'Hut Tax.' Whatever your District Officer's decision is, let us know: We will take it from there."

He got up, marched into his hut leaving the policeman sitting on his stool.

Five days after Thomas' return, the District Officer ordered a Senior Tax Collector to collect the 'Hut Tax' from the Chiefdom at whatever cost. He allocated a contingent of eight Tax Collectors and thirty armed policemen who left for Bureh's Chiefdom. Word of their departure preceded them, through the bush telephone, by about three days.

Awaiting their arrival, the Chief imprisoned his Senior Adviser and the Witchdoctor and had his resident male subjects, both young and old, prepare for the eventuality of any fighting.

The District Officials arrived on a beautiful, warm, sunny day: Swallows darted playfully in the clear blue sky, and the chatter of monkeys cascaded down from nearby forests.

They were received, as befitting government officials, with respect and honor. The trouble began when they insisted on collecting the 'Tax.'

"Why must we pay your 'Hut Tax?" The Chief demanded. "When you came to our lands, you met us living in our huts. We didn't have your help in building them nor in their upkeep, now. We see no reason to pay your 'Hut Tax."

The senior of the Tax Collectors was uneasy. He'd noticed that all of the Chief's Officials had their war clothes on and carried weapons. Worse still, the two he could have depended on were nowhere in sight.

"We were ordered to collect the tax, Chief," he said. "In the event you refuse to pay it, you'll be taken to the District Head-quarters then to Freetown in chains."

The Chief asked if they were in the position to do that. Didn't he think it was arrogant for them, with so few men, to consider taking him to their Head-quarters in chains?

The Officer went red in the face. He was one, like the District Officer, who thought all black men were their inferiors. He wasn't gong to take lip from a savage; he'd been sent to collect taxes and, by-gum, he'd do just that.

"Don't make trouble, Chief," he said. "You people must pay the 'Hut Tax' or stand the consequences!"

Bureh drew on his beard then pointed to a window.

"Look toward the palisade," he said.

He did as was suggested: The palisade was lined—two deep—on the inside by men armed mostly with Shakabullahs, but a few carried spears or bows and arrows.

"See why you can't threaten us?" the Chief asked.

The warriors broke into a war song and began circling the palisade in a frenzied dance while letting out blood-chilling cries that stood the officer's hairs on their ends.

They were in trouble: Thomas and he had argued for more than the thirty men they had been given for protection; the D.O. had disagreed. They were outnumbered by at least five to one.

The dancers tightened their circle about the Chief's hut. They had gotten midway between it and the palisade when the sounds of shots came from around the hut where the armed police had stationed themselves.

Three of the dancers threw up their hands then fell to the ground. Taking what cover they could find, those of Bureh's men with guns, and bows and arrows returned the fire. The spear carriers charged forward screaming their hate: They were mown down like dogs.

The Senior Tax official and Thomas, prisoners within the Chief's hut, could do nothing to stop the fight: They couldn't appeal to the Chief and his High Officials who were at the windows and doors shooting at the police from the rear.

An hour passed before the fighting subsided. The smoke cleared to show twelve District officers were dead (including the sergeant in charge of the fighting contingent).

Many more lay around the hut mortally wounded. Twenty-one of The Chief's men lay sprawled and lifeless about the courtyard. The healthy were administering to their injured compatriots.

The Senior Tax Collector, Thomas, and the government men still on their feet were rounded up, stripped of their weapons and outer garments then released into the surrounding forests with their injured and dead.

The Chief and his Elders were aware of the implications of the day's events: There was no turning back now. The White man's blood had been spilt. They would return with larger numbers and better arms and munitions to exact revenge. They wouldn't be satisfied until the Chief, his Elders and the war boys were all captured or killed. Maybe, even the Chiefdom would be razed to the ground.

Bureh wondered if the situation was that terrible.

"Once in a People's lifetime," he said to those around him, "a stand must be made over some matter. This 'Hut Tax' is ours."

"Our People are with you in the matter, Chief," the Acting Senior Adviser said.

"Their men are better trained and they use superior weapons. But, if we can't die resisting payment of taxes on our huts, what type of men are we?" Bureh asked. "Bring out the talking drums: Send out messages to the Chiefdoms harboring our men. Tell them to return immediately with their arms and munitions. In another fortnight, we'd have a war on our hands.

# Tainted Revenge

In the name of Allah, the magnificent, the almighty, the merciful, may the souls of these wretched dogs who this day defile my body be damned and burn in hell.

Grabs your heart, don't it? Makes you wonder why a human being would condemn fellow beings to such an end. Being dragged toward an isolated grove of Baobab trees by dozens of angry, gesticulating women—some frothing at the mouth—all screaming for some harm to be done to me, would. Don't you think so?

The rabble and I made our way to the opening in the grove, with its matting of damp, decaying leaves, as my struggles reached fever pitch. I could see, by the light of the moon, a rope of plaited hemp—with a wicked looking noose at its business end.

It hung from the lowest branch of a tree—about sixty feet high—and swung ever so gently in a breeze. Underneath was a stone—three feet high by two feet wide.

My heart beat violently and my feet trembled.

My mouth became infused with bile; I spat most out but choked as some flowed down my windpipe. My unshod right foot came to life and connected with a face: A cry arose from one of those at the lower half of my person; it pleased me no end. The pleasure was short lived, though: Someone grabbed my testes and savagely wrung them. The pressure on my right leg returned—applied by two pairs of hoe-hardened hands—effectively keeping it out of the fray.

"Let go!" I screamed hoping my voice would carry, in the warm October night, to our village, Rotifunk'. "What you are doing is evil and downright illegal. You aren't the law."

I could feel the perspiration on my body being wafted away, by a breeze, cooling it down.

"Save it. No one can hear you," said a voice at my head while a palm descended over my mouth snuffing out my protests.

The only sounds during the remainder of the journey were those of a Solitary owl and the ominous crunch of dozens of feet on the leaf-strewn enclave that held the instruments of my death.

You may wonder how I got into this crisis. Three days earlier, citizens of the village (I am a Councilor) brought me before the Paramount Chief of the Chiefdom.

Chief, Issa Dura, new at the time, asked what the charges against me were. My case was the first he sat in judgment on: The court barray was overflowing. For a minute or two, there was complete silence during which the citizens eyed one another taking comfort from the look on each other's faces.

It was broken by a rasping voice which I recognized immediately.

"Chief," it said, "he be accused for not bathing for many years. He smells like an un-emptied latrine. Can't you smell him?"

It was the voice of Mariama, the senior wife of a rival woodcutter. It carried to the corners of the barray and, for a while, it overpowered the murmur of disapproval that was making its way through the assembled.

For a barray, the assembly was colorful; it came from the

female members of the Chiefdom who were sitting, in force, at the front rows. They were attired in their Friday-best: Long flowing, colorful, light-cotton-gara gowns over weaved, heavy-cotton lappas. Their heads were wrapped in huge, variously tied materials that matched their lappas. This display of colors was overlooked by the men who, I think, understood that this was the first time they—the women—were being active participants in such proceedings.

The women, on the other hand, hadn't this understanding. A current of expectancy lurked just beneath their veneer of festivity. They wanted justice not only done, but to be seen to be done. They knew their men; they watched for any of their high-handed tricks and were determined to beat them, soundly, at their own game. They would prove that my pong and it alone was the cause of the deaths and other mishaps in their villages.

The expectancy and festivity ended at the first row carrying the men. They sat immediately behind their womenfolk on this occasion: The Chief decreed so; it was an important day in the lives of their mates, mothers, sisters, and daughters. As usual, most had on dull, drab, cotton vests and the remainder heavy cotton-woven Ronkos with matching caps. For pants, it was every man on his own: The ones matching their tops being prevalent but some with gabardine pants many of which were faded and almost in tatters.

Most sympathized with their women folk's viewpoint on this particular issue. However, they feared the new found aggression their women displayed. In the olden days, no woman would jeopardize her position in the community by leveling such charges against a man, even if he warranted it. That was the duty of the husband, if she was married, a father, a brother or some other male relative if not. They watched Allah's-given rights to them being slowly eroded. If they knew anything about women, and they felt they did, they would be second class citizens before things completely settled down.

I took some time of these thoughts to scrutinize the new Paramount Chief; he really was a dashing figure. Though sitting on a low copper stool, he towered above most of his courtiers. He looked thirty-five maybe thirty-six. He'd done well at the 'School for the Sons of Chiefs', at Bo then left the Chiefdom for Fourah Bay College, in Freetown, when he turned eighteen amid speculations of his ever returning. For years after that, all we'd heard about him was he'd earned a first degree and had gone overseas to study 'The Law.'

Maybe, he hadn't meant things to get this far, so quickly on his becoming Paramount Chief at the death of his father. Maybe, he'd thought he would ease the changes, into the Chiefdom, over a period of several years. One would imagine he hoped to enlighten the populace, especially the men, about the complexities of the Whiteman's ways. However, he reckoned without the women's connivance and determination: Things had gone completely out of his control and they were slowly taken over the running of our villages and towns.

Some of the latter saw that I was watching them: They grabbed their noses and fanned the air around them with the palms of their hands. Soon, loud mutterings and angry gestures came from where they sat.

"Order," the Court Messenger shouted. "There must be order in this Court."

The assembly fell silent. I faced the chief. We gazed at each other for a while.

"How do you plead?" He asked grabbing at his copper coronet as it was won't to slip down to his ears, every so often. "Won't you say something? He said when I didn't reply. "You're in great trouble, here. How did you get yourself into this mess?"

"People in our villages envy me," I said realizing I would have landed in big trouble if I didn't reply this time around. "They want to bring me down."

This elicited a loud hiss from somewhere. I faced that direction to find the hate-filled face of my accuser.

"Stupid dog," she said taking a white head-tie from her bosom and holding it to her nose. "Nobody want to bring you down. You are all ready below ground."

"Order," The Court Messenger shouted. "I want order in this court."

"His pong has caused plenty of trouble in the village, Chief," said Mariama ignoring the Messenger's order. However, she fell quiet when the Chief held up his right hand.

After he adjusted his coronet, which had fallen down to his ears, again, he turned to his Chief Adviser and asked, "How long hasn't he taken a bath?

The Adviser started counting the fingers of his left hand missed and started over.

Getting to the fourth, this time around, he stopped.

"Four years, Chief," he said. His voice carried a tinge of awe. "He hasn't taken a bath for four years. Yes, Chief." he continued, "he hasn't washed for four years. That's why he smell so bad."

The Chief nodded. The coronet wobbled then fell to his ears. He let it stay, turned to his Adviser and asked why the case had not been brought up earlier.

"The accused," he said, "couldn't have smelled any more or less three years and nine months before that day."

The Adviser suppressed a laugh. Some action had been taken he said. The accused had been brought before the Alpha (Priest) of his village's Moslem community.

I remembered that four years earlier I had stood in front of our Alpha.

"A major dictate of Islam," he'd admonished, "was cleanliness. A devout Moslem had to pray five times a day. Each prayer should be preceded by the cleansing of oneself in body and spirit."

He shouldn't worry, I replied. Although I smelled to high heaven, I happened to be a good Moslem. I prayed the stipulated times per day. Also, wasn't the given of alms, to the poor a dictate of Islam: Well, no one was better at it than me in the village.

The Alpha had been worried by my argument.

"Living in my village and not taking a bath will force me to expel you from our Jamat," he had said.

This had caused me to say something which I don't recall at this time and I had walked out of his presence.

"Everyone hoped that the Alpha's words would put some sense into his head at the time, Chief," the Adviser said. "It didn't happen; things get even worse: He refused to launder his clothes."

"That's the truth, Chief," Mariama said. "The smell got so bad, after the second year, our Alpha got angry; he expelled him from the Jamat. On the third year," she continued after thinking for a while, "his wife, Isatu, left taking their children with her to stay with her parents at Waterloo near Freetown."

"Have they not returned?" the Chief asked.

"Would you return if it was you, Chief?" The Adviser asked looking stunned. "This man wore the same clothes—day and night—for two years. They got so tattered and torn it was the dirt that kept them from falling off his back."

The Chief asked why I let things slide so much. He hoped it wasn't due to laziness.

I told him it wasn't. On most days, I got up before five in the morning. This gave me some hours' advantage over most of my competition in coal making.

This raised the Chief's eyebrows. He turned to the Adviser and asked if I had become lucky or wealthy of late.

The voice of Mariama, she who knew everything, said I had become prosperous over the last three years. All the neighboring villages bought their fire-wood and coal from me. Using trickery, I had eliminated my rivals.

The Chief seemed amused.

"Do I detect some jealousy, here?" he asked. "He seems to work very hard."

"No Chief," she said. "He does not work harder than my husband; why should he be this lucky?"

"Maybe," the Chief said giving the Adviser a barbed stare—his hand had wandered toward his toppled coronet—"his methods for producing charcoal are cheaper and quicker. Maybe, he worships the Devil. Get your husband to investigate and copy his ways."

"We don't do Devil Worship, Chief," she said

"You must have done something else to make him change his ways?" The Chief asked his Adviser his nose wrinkling.

"He was taken before his Section Chief," the Adviser replied. "He gave him the same excuses he gave the Alpha. The arguments the Section Chief countered with were wasted on him."

"What did the Section Chief do?"

"He ordered that he was bound and washed in the river." The Adviser said after some thought. "Also, he ordered that new clothes were given to him."

"Was that done?"

"Yes, Chief," Mariama answered.

Chief turned to her.

"Did it help? What else did the Section Chief do?"

"It did for a while, Chief. After a few weeks, the men lost

interest; they didn't get him to wash regularly nor get him to change the clothes they gave him: Soon, he smelled worse than before."

"Things fell apart then, Chief," the Adviser said.

"What happened?" The Chief asked.

"Strange things started, Chief," cried Mariama before the Adviser could answer.

"Children died in our village; huts burned to the ground, and our animals died suddenly."

"The carelessness of the mothers," the Chief said, "as their children played with matches—unsupervised—may have caused the fires. You have no proof he started them."

"But Chief, three, four years back," the Adviser said, "such things didn't happen; nor did the sicknesses that are now in our village."

"Large numbers of our children die," Mariama said. "Dysentery, measles, and pneu—pneu—"

"You mean pneumonia?" the Chief said.

"Yes, Chief," she said. "These are the problems we have. One of mine died last year."

"I cannot be blamed for that," I said. "Children would have died even if I bathed every second of our waking day. Didn't villages around us have deaths before ours did?"

"I don't know," she said. "All I know is that the children die after you stopped bathing and washing your clothes."

The Chief raised his eyebrows.

"Children died in Waterloo and surrounding villages before any did in Rotufunk', didn't they?" he asked. "Our Chief Medical Officer, in his report, said so. The bacteria and virus must have been brought to your villages from Waterloo—and its surrounding villages—by your visiting relatives and friends."

"Bacteria, Virus? We know nothing about them, Chief. We

know," she pointed at me, "he worships the Devil who kill our offspring and our animals."

"If anyone dies, it should be him," Chief said. "He's covered in filth. Illnesses should be attracted to him."

He grabbed at his wayward coronet.

Mariama with legs spread-eagled and arms akimbo faced him.

"That Chief," she said, "is Whiteman thinking. We are black people: Africans. This is witchcraft: Not British Medicine or British Law."

"Easy, now, Mariama," whispered the women standing by her as a hush descended on the barray. "You don't want to get the Chief angry. He has experience in such things."

"Damn the Chief," she shouted. "What experience?" Her finger pointed at him.

"Because you come from England, you think you know everything. Well, let me tell you something, Chief, you know nothing. You've been away for so long that you forgot most of our customs and ways."

Sniggers were hurriedly smothered where the men sat.

"Tell it like you see it, sister," a voice—from way back—boomed. "Make Chief know the way you feel."

"In this barray, woman, no one; I repeat, no one will accuse me of being unfair," the Chief said. "All you've done is made accusations. I want evidence, woman; evidence showing that his not bathing killed your children. If his spouse and children had died while living with him that might have been some form of evidence. As it is, there is no evidence to show it was his smell and filth that killed the children in your houses. Did he sleep in the houses of any of those who died?"

The Chief Adviser said no.

"You had relatives, from nearby villages, who might have been carrying the bacteria and virus sleeping in your homes, didn't you?"

The answer was yes.

"That's where the illnesses came from; not from some unwashed scoundrel. In my view, being kicked out of his Jamat and losing his family were enough punishment for his actions."

"That isn't fair, Chief," she said. "Our laws say he must die: That's the only way our children can live."

"The laws have changed," Chief said shaking his head. "The deaths in the villages could be prevented by people boiling the water they drink; keeping their villages well swept, clean, and by behaving like responsible human beings by not peeing and defecating everywhere."

"How can we do that, Chief?" the Adviser asked.

"Every last Saturday in the month," he said, "would be, 'Village Cleaning,' day. Villagers would be responsible for cleaning their homes, their surroundings, and their roads. Also, during each month, mothers should take their offspring to the hospital when they are ill instead of seeing their respective witchdoctors. By the end of this month, each hut must have a latrine dug. If not, its owner would be fined for every day it's without one."

"Won't that put the Chiefdom's business backward, Chief?" his Adviser asked.

"This is the Chiefdom's business, too. But, if that is the price the Chiefdom pays for good health and the lives of its young, then so be it."

"People will refuse to carry out the clean up," Mariama said. "As for going to your hospital, I don't know a woman who would do so."

"Clean up would be from seven to ten-thirty in the mornings," the Chief said.

"Anyone on the roads—not cleaning and picking up litter—before then, would be fined one hundred Leones and put in jail for a week. If a child falls ill and dies, in the care of the witchdoctor, its parents and the doctor will be charged and brought to the courts. If they are found guilty, of neglect, they would be jailed for a year, each. This is the law of the land, now."

"Locking us up won't do any good. What happens when our children die of malnutrition, as most of them do?" A female voice asked. "Would we still be placed in jail?"

"That's another matter: It will be resolved in the near future," the Chief said. He turned to me. "You're banished from the village until you can show me and the Chief Adviser, here, you bathe regularly. You will occupy one of the leper-huts outside your village until that time."

Mariama turned abruptly from the Chief and stormed out of the barray.

"Don't depend on the Chief's words," she flung at me as she swept out. "We'll get you for this. We, the women, run this Chiefdom, now. We will find a way to do away with you."

I was taken to the leper huts which were situated about two miles away from our village so that I wouldn't continue to contaminate my fellow villagers.

I awoke to the whispers of female voices three nights later. A boney knee straddled my chest: It belonged to my erstwhile enemy, Mariama. While she pinned me to the bed, several calloused hands undressed me. They then grabbed my naked body and hoisted it into the air aided by several others. With a cry that could have raised the dead, I was rushed out of the hut into the morning air which, even though warm, caused me to shiver.

We stopped under the Baobab Tree. I was dumped on my feet then frog marched to where Mariama waited pulling on the rope and caressing its noose.

"Have you anything to say?" She asked. "I said you shouldn't rely on the Chief's words; it's us, women who run this Chiefdom now."

Our eyes locked for a while during which I felt cold fingers running along my spine and a pressure developing within my scrotum. I saw her for what she was: An old hag who watched life pass her husband and herself by. I came along and did better than they had in the 'Charcoal Making Trade.' She set out to get me.

"Why these women look up to you for any decision making is beyond me," I said straining on the stone on which I now stood. "You are nothing but an old slut with alcohol for blood and sawdust for brains. My dog won't take advice from you. Your husband—poor man—should have married a woman from Freetown, a Boraka (A non-Bundo woman).

Her friends tittered.

She walked closer to stand in front of me.

"Are you not afraid to die?" She asked. "Don't you feel death embracing you, yet you insult me?"

She placed the noose around my neck and adjusted it.

"If I was you, I will shut up and keep my breath for what I am about to go through," she said moving away from me.

I laughed.

"What does your husband see in you?" I asked. "You lied about losing a child at the Chief's barray. Everyone in our village knows you have no children; no man would want a child with you. The one animal that would give you a child would be a baboon, maybe."

I could feel my penis threatening to overflow with urine.

Her screams savaged the morning's calm. They startled the owl in its perch; as its wings beat on the air, Mariama lunched herself at me her mouth wide open.

The pressure in my scrotum had by now increased beyond

bursting but I held it in check. Meanwhile, I threw a few more taunts her way and willed her to position herself just right. Soon, she was standing directly beneath me her mouth open in a yawn-like scream. Taking as near-a-perfect aim as I could—tottering on the slab of stone—I sent a stream of warm urine into her face.

She gasped; her hands flew to her throat which moved involuntarily. Rage replaced the surprise on her face as she stuck the fingers of her right hand into her mouth.

I laughed like the damned: It ended abruptly; the noose tightening around my throat: The stone had been pushed from underneath me, leaving me thrashing about on the rope. As I watched—through tear filled eyes—she fought to expel my pee from her system.

I had only a few minutes to live, now. On the other hand, she had years to do so, maybe. Everyone there knew I'd had the last laugh: I put my curse on her. I owned her body and soul; her mind was mine to mess with from the grave.

# Supplanted Wife

Think of the brilliant sun dipping beyond a shimmering river that reflected its colors of oranges, reds, and blues. Imagine its intense heat giving way to a cool breeze that blew from one forested knoll to another while caressing the brown, hard-packed earth. Then, think of long tendrils of darkness snaking their way through the remaining light of a once glorious day. There, you have it: Ending of the day in a Sierra Leonean town.

At the outskirts of one such town, M'forki, a family—a man playing with a child, a woman, and three girls—sat in front of their hut enjoying the warm mango-and-guava-scented breeze that blew over their small farm holding.

Yahbom, a woman of about thirty-five years, watched her husband, Tommy; toss the child—a boy of about two—into the air. Her face was troubled; she closed her eyes to keep from seeing the love in the face of her spouse. If he caught the boy one more time, then kiss him on the jaw, she thought, she would scream.

"I hope he drops him, he hits his head and he becomes crippled," she said to herself as he sent the boy into the air and caught him. "My girls will get back the father's love they lost. Why don't he bond with my girls anymore? Is it because they are older?

That is true, but they have grown to an age when girls need a father's love the most."

She sighed. Why was she raging against the boy? She shouldn't hate him. He didn't do anything to her. It wasn't his fault his father behaved the way he did to her and his siblings. If anyone was at fault, it was that witch-of-a-mother of his.

Mariama—the boy's mother—had come along in their (Tommy's and hers) sixteenth year of marriage, as a second wife; she was just seventeen then. Before she appeared, she could always come up with ways to keep him from marrying other women, especially those that were younger than her. He'd married a few that were older but they had not given him an offspring let alone a boy: They'd been sent packing. The seventeen-year old came along in their sixteenth year of marriage bliss and was able to withstand her many machinations. Then, out of pure spite, it seemed, the young she-devil bore Tommy the son he had been praying and hoping for.

"Why couldn't it have been me?" She mused while trying to block out the happy chuckles of the boy and his father's voice that sang him a lullaby. "I slave all these years to make my Tommy a happy man; when things begin to go my way, the boy appears.

Now, he won't provide the necessary things for my girls to complete their schooling. When they get to the marrying age, he will pack them off to some old men if their bride prices are right."

"Years ago, I should have stuck with one of my second wives," he said.

She came out of her reverie and looked in his direction; the boy had fallen asleep in his father's arms.

"Her sons would be giving me plenty help in my farm now," he continued. "You couldn't stand mates, you told me. Those that I married you either beat or had the witchdoctor removed. You even had one abort her five months' pregnancy."

"That wasn't my fault," she said wiping her eyes. "For one who don't believe in witchcraft you have some funny ideas. You know she slipped and fell down the hospital steps."

"Family members who were there said otherwise. You give me daughters; girls who go to school. If they learn Domestic Science and can collect water and firewood they will be of use around here and to me especially."

She gave a bemused smile.

"The boy is two," she said. "When he is five and ready for school, see if his mother don't talk you into sending him. What will you do? Kick them out of their home? Beat her so she die?"

"No son of mine will attend the white-man's school," he said his menacing look finally silencing her. "He'll work with me on my farm making a living and learning at the same time. The only book he is going to study is the Koran."

"You say so now," she said. "Three years is a short time to wait: We'll see then." She rose and gave a loud yawn. "I have a terrible headache. Come on girls let's go indoors so you can do your homework and I can take a rest."

She could see that Fattu, the youngest of her three girls, was restless. She pulled her close and asked what was troubling her.

"I did my homework, Mama," she said. "Can't I stay out here with Dad? I don't feel at all sleepy."

"No, you are going in with me," she said pulling her toward the hut by an arm. "You need to sleep: You have to go to school in the morning."

"Leave her with me," her husband's voice stopped her in her tracks. "It is only seven in the evening; I'll bring her to you in an hour."

"Damn you, Tommy," She raged storming into the hut followed by the other girls.

"Think you can turn me youngest against me? That won' happen; I'll see you in hell, first: Just you wait and see."

She slammed the door to her hut. A wave of hot pungent air assailed her nostrils as she walked into her bedroom. She pushed open the window letting in some cool, fruit-scented breeze.

How she hated the room: It was mosquito laden and, worst of all, one could see the moon and stars through the roof. On rainy days, torrents of water cascaded through it to soak her bed and other furniture. Why did he move her out of the new hut he'd built her? Just so that child-witch could move in with her boy? She'd prostituted her dignity and begged: He refused to build a bigger hut for her and the girls. That virago has one boy and she gets a four-room hut for her own.

She supervised the changing of the girl's clothing an hour later. She then undressed in the vastly cooled room then draped a clean, flowery lappa, anchored around her neck, by a knot, over her flagging breasts. She lay on the bed intending to rest for a short while. The next thing she knew daylight was streaming into the room.

Utter dejection dampened her spirit: Starting on Sunday, it would be her week to prepare Tommy's food; he would stay in her hut during this time. She didn't love doing this anymore: He didn't bring home the monkey-and-deer meat that he haunted.

"This is all I could catch," he said tossing the carcass of an emaciated squirrel at her feet on the Sunday evening. "There is not much to hunt in the forest these days." His breath reeked of alcohol.

"You could not find a groundhog or rabbit?" She asked grabbing her nose. "Oh, I see; you left those with your son's mother. Won' you toss me a rabbit someday? I do make wonderful rabbit stews, you know."

He laughed derisively.

"I give Mariama the rabbits because she takes care of my boy. I want him to be strong when he grows up. If you want to prepare rabbit stew, again, give me a son or go haunt rabbits yourself."

Her eyes smoldered.

"One day," she said flinging the carcass at his retreating form, "you'll see that my girls are important, too, and that Mariama don' love you like I do."

"As if I care," he said. "She could leave tonight: She'll do so without my boy who you'd have to care for. Now, where's my food."

"You must be crazy. I won't care for him. Did you provide the things to prepare food for you? If you want food, I've got my goat-hide slippers under the bed that you could—"

Her mouth snapped shut from a slap.

"I won't take any lip from you," he said. "You are going to prepare some food for me even if you do the hunting yourself. If not, I'll give you a good beating."

He returned home on the Tuesday without any meat from which she could make a stew.

She killed and cooked the leanest of her ducks that roamed the yard around her hut after a noisy burst up. She had been saving them—and about two dozen chickens—for the days in March when the intense heat prevented husbands from bringing bush meat to their spouses for food.

"See what a little talking to can do," he taunted as he tucked into the breast of the duck. "I must do that more often; it would give me great pleasure and knock some sense into your stupid head."

The berated woman silently endured the taunts.

"One of these days," she seethed quietly, "I'll put a stop to this madness. He isn't going to eat us out of the food I have put aside for the days when times are rough."

She was forced to prepare a few more of the poultry she raised during the rest of that week. With each bird killed, her resentment toward him welled up.

And it continued during early March, when the days became blast furnaces and the nights not much cooler. Old folks and the very young died from the intense heat as from the lack of food and water it caused.

During the second week of the month when it became her turn to entertain her husband, she had two of the ducks and all of the chickens she depended on to feed the girls. She waited with bated breath for Tommy's appearance and the unbridled arguments and verbal torture she knew would come on the Sunday.

Numerous ways of avoiding these came to her mind but none panned out. Whiskey, Tommy's hunting dog, hanging around the doors of her hut, early on the Sunday of their stay, put an end to these thoughts.

It took a lot of courage and nerve for the plan to be carried out; her spouse dotted on the stupid mutt. Whiskey was special and had been his main hunting dog for over four years, now: They went everywhere and understood each other perfectly.

She eventually trapped the animal after several bites and slit its throat. What would her fate be, if Tommy found out? She wondered. Within the next hour, she had the carcass dismembered and cleaned. The innards, meat, and skin were cooked into what was, to her mind, the best stew she could prepare under the circumstances. The limbs, ears, tail, and head she dumped in holes over which she planted pepper, okra, and cassava shoots in a garden at the back of her hut.

She nervously watched her husband eat his dinner that evening. She needn't have worried: He had second and third helpings. At the meal's end, he assembled the children at the front door of the hut to render old songs and relate tall stories of bygone days while she quietly looked on.

March sailed along with the village's problems worsening. For one, the sun's heat sapped the energy of the hunters especially men like Tommy in their late forties. Also, the groundhogs and rabbits took to staying in their burrows refusing to surface until late in the cool of the evenings.

In Tommy's case, however, things were even worse: He missed the one item which made him the excellent hunter he was, Whisky. He'd searched extensively for his hunting companion during the days following that sumptuous meal at Yahbom's: They failed to turn up the dog. Maybe, it had been eaten by wild animals or it had simply run away because of Mariama's persistent berating and several beatings were the consensus. If either of the two was the case, he had little hope of ever seeing his comrade again.

Despondent during the following days, he could only take Mariama—whose week it was to prepare his food—the squirrels he bagged so she could cook for his son.

She threatened to take the boy to his grandparents' home at M'forki. Her father, she insinuated, was a remarkable hunter, a better provider of food, and a superior man to him.

His senior spouse made do—during these hard times—with the ducks and chicken she saved supplementing them with the flesh of rodents she caught in traps set around her hut. Also, she prepared the flesh of reptiles for the children to eat for the first time.

She prayed that Mariama would carry out her threat and visit her parents.

Her next period of entertaining Tommy started with the family watching vultures soaring in the sky, in front of her hut, on hot thermal currents then dive only to rise, gracefully, and continue their search for carrion.

"Pa Tommy," a young girl's voice broke into this period of bonding.

Yahbom looked up: It was Menna, her mate's younger sister, she was running toward them.

"Come quick," she cried, "Mariama's baby vomit and sweat. He will toilet himself to death."

Tommy looked over at his senior wife.

"You can go," she said. "But I want you back after you see the doctor. If not, I will come to her hut and get you."

He promised to do so as he walked off towards his younger wife's hut. He didn't show up at his senior wife's until the Wednesday evening of that week.

"Is your son all right?" She asked as he entered the hut. "Was the child so sick that you spend three of my days with that person?"

"The boy had a fever and dysentery," he said. "We went to the doctor's hut on each of those days. I didn't care to leave him."

She smiled as she wiped the sweat off her face.

"You used my three days without my permission?" She asked. "Look, Mister, you have other children to love and feed. These days, it is 'The Boy', 'The Boy'; you don' pay much attention to my girls."

"So?"

"Your absence is a problem," she said. "On two occasions, times when you should have been with them, you did not show up: Something about taking the boy to his grandparents' village. They cried themselves to sleep every day through out those two weeks. Tommy, do you ever think about our children? They may be girls but they miss you. They need the love and time of their father, too."

"I love my daughters," he said, "but not as much as I do my son. They won't carry my name into the future."

"That may be true. But, they are still your children. When they grow up, they'll give you plenty grandchildren: Isn't that something to look forward to?"

"It is. My son, though, will carry on my line and give me grandchildren, too. Through him, there will be male Bangura's in the generations after him. That is not possible with your girls: Their children will carry the names of other men. My line will be lost forever with them."

"You have nephews who have carried on your father's line; isn't that enough for you? And, who say the boy will give you grandchildren? He may like men. Anyway, husband, be careful: Be very careful. Strange things have happened to children who are shown so much love."

"Don't threaten my son, woman," he said towering over her. "He was sick. I had to be there to comfort him. I will take one week even one year of your time if that's what is necessary for him to get well. I am the boss in this family."

"You've got three offspring—from two wives before me—they are all females. She comes along and her first child is a boy: Don't that tell you something? Don't you see she took advantage of the feelings of a stupid and foolish, old man?"

A single blow landed her on the floor. She was then trussed up—like a Christmas Turkey—with deer-hide ropes. She was dumped on her bedroom floor where, every so often, her tormentor poured cups of hot water on the ropes. The water would slowly evaporate contracting the latter evoking anguished cries of pain from their prisoner.

Their offspring pleaded with the incensed father, as the torture extended into the early evening, to no avail. The oldest, on her mother's advice, went from hut to hut soliciting the villagers help. She failed to find any until she got to the Chief's who came with her to put an end to the suffering.

Over the next month, Tommy was noticeably absent at Yahbom's. He didn't provide food for her family, either. On the fifth week of his absence, she walked over to her mate's hut.

"What's she doing here?" The lady of the hut asked on opening her front door and seeing her rival standing there. "Tell her not to step into my hut unless she gets my permission."

She was told not to pester her mate. Wouldn't she go to her hut if she hadn't seen him for over a month? He then turned to his senior spouse.

"Come in, come into the hut. You are not here to cause more trouble?" He asked. "I hope not. You should have learned from what happened at your place last month."

"I don't care what happened between the two of you a month ago," the junior spouse said standing within the frame of the doorway blocking her mate's entrance into the hut. "If you two must talk, you do so in the yard."

"Oh, Allah," he said as he squeezed by her and walked out.

The sight of him walking outdoors brought a sly smile to Yahbom's face.

"Now, who is the boss in that hut?" She asked as they walked away. "She treats you like a dog. Why do you put up with it? Is it because of her son? Why don't you come home where you belong, to people who love and respect you?"

Her husband smiled.

"Why do you treat us this way?" She continued. "The children miss you. They can't visit when you are in her hut. The other village women laugh and make fun of me. They say I cannot compete with a mere child: I learn nothing from our Society."

"Tell the kids that I love them," he said. 'Say I'll see them very soon."

"You can come over and see them, now," she said.

"I'll only do so when you behave better toward me."

She grabbed hold of his arm and hung on to it as he fought to free it.

"Is that the real reason? Isn't it because she told you not to come?"

Freeing his hand he quickly walked to the hut. He returned to hers a week later.

"What, no food?" He protested on his arrival. "Your duty is to have my meal on the table whenever I am in this hut. A man needs his nourishments to live."

"His children and wife too," she said. "I didn't know you were coming. Where is the meat of the game birds and muskrats you hunted? Other husbands bring them home for their wives to prepare. You don't even bring fish from the river for your children."

"I hate fishing," he said frowning. "I won't spend my time doing it. Also, I don't have the money to buy some for you people."

She shrugged. Whether he went fishing or bought some fish didn't matter, she thought.

"You eat in this hut when you provide the food," she said. "For someone who say he hates fishing, and can't buy any fish, you do a good job taking them to your slut of a second wife."

His rush landed them both on the floor.

"She isn't a slut," he raged. "She prepares my meals whenever I am with her."

"That's because you give her all the meat you can find," she said.

"You'll prepare food for me or else."

He turned to see the children watching them.

"Now, woman, I want a good meal when I come home tomorrow. It must be a nice fish-ball stew," he said getting from on top of her.

"Where am I to get the fish?" she asked.

He didn't care how she got the fish neither what type it was. On his return home the next day, he wanted some fish-ball stew on the table. He turned away and stalked toward the front door grumbling.

"No, Dada," wailed their oldest child, "don't leave. You've been away for too long; we've missed you so much. Mama has no more food for us; she's been preparing rodents and snakes for us to eat. You have to provide us with something to eat."

She landed on the floor with the shake of her father's arm. The younger kids seeing their sibling on the floor ran to her and they huddled together whimpering.

"Please Tommy," their mother pleaded, "don't hurt the children. It will ruin their young lives. For their sakes, I will prepare your food. Just don't hurt them."

He glared at her.

"I hope you know better not to talk back in front of them from now on," he said as he retreated from the whimpering group.

His first wife went fishing the next morning. It was a wasted day. Having nothing to prepare his food she waited for his return fearing for hers and their children's lives. She thought of ways of preparing different stews with the remaining chickens she'd been saving for sacrifices to Masala (the god that gave women male children) and food for the children. She decided that it wasn't worth the trouble.

She watched Tommy stagger home in the early evening that day. He made for the kitchen the minute he arrived instead of taking a bath.

"Yahbom," he bellowed, "where is my food? You promised to do whatever I asked."

The poor woman said she had not prepared any food. She had gone to the river but came back empty handed. She had nothing in the hut with which to prepare food for him.

"Damn you, woman," he said, "I want to eat now. Where are the chickens you have running all over the yard? Prepare one for me."

"You are drunk," she said, "not crazy. Will Mariama cook offerings to her God for your dinner? I am saving them for something more important than food for you."

He took about six paces toward her then keeled over: He'd been tripped by a long-stem broom held by the girls. He ranted and raved for the remainder of the evening but had to make do with a bowl of boiled cassava topped with palm oil and pepper for a late dinner.

Yahbom awoke the next morning with a determined set to her chin. She boiled cassava, sprinkled palm oil and cayenne pepper over them and handed each child a bowl with a cup of unsweetened, milk-less tea. After they left for school, she hurried to the river. She hadn't a minnow to show after four hours of effort, by noon. She returned home with bizarre thoughts of the beatings to come and how she might elude them.

She spent the next two hours contemplating the matter. At around three o'clock, as she sat fanning herself with a breadfruit leaf, she saw her mate's son stumble out of their hut to play in the dusty yard. She watched, bewildered, as he grabbed a handful of earth then brought it toward his mouth. She got up and was running toward him hoping she got there in time.

"Boy, you must not eat dirt," she said when she was by his side. "Where is your mother, anyway?"

"What's it to you if he eats dirt?" a voice within her said. "Here's the God-given chance to even things up between his mother and yourself."

She couldn't believe what she had thought of doing. She hurried toward her mate's hut to find its front door wide open. Walking in, moving from room to room calling, "Mariama, Menna?" No one answered.

"You see?" the voice said. "There is no one home. What type of mother leaves a two-year old alone in a hut? Go on, do what I suggested."

She walked out of the hut the boy in her arms. She couldn't do what her conscience dictated: The child had done her no wrong.

"Well, that is correct," the voice said, "but Tommy provided him with fish, yesterday. Did he do that for your girls? No? Yet, he wanted you to prepare fish-ball stew for him. Where were you to get the fish for the balls?"

"Remember," the voice persisted, "he told you that his possessions that would have gone to your girls are now the boy's. They'll be destitute; they'll end up married to old, senile men. When they've gone, you'll become a discarded woman: Someone no other man will look at."

She still couldn't bring herself to do the dastardly deed. How could she live with such a terrible thing for the rest of her life?

"Miss this chance," the voice said, "and you had better disappear taking your kids with you. But, where can you hide? You'll have to murder your children and then commit suicide yourself."

The thought of destroying her children finally overcame her resistance.

Raw meat was soon being pounded in a mortar. As the tender flesh was pulverized into paste, her remorse was partially expunged by torrents of uncontrolled tears. She fashioned the paste into balls which she deep fried in palm oil. She had begun singing, not so heartily, when her mate burst into the kitchen.

Their eyes locked for a brief moment.

"Damn you, Mariama. Must you burst into my kitchen like this?" She asked as old hatreds and animosities arose within her. "Don't you know to knock? You need my permission to enter this hut."

"Forgive me, Yahbom," her mate said gasping for breath. "I am in big trouble; have you seen the boy?"

Her mate felt some compassion for her but it lasted for only a brief second.

"No," she said. "I just come back from the river. Where was he?"

She had left him playing in her hut while she dashed to her garden for some vegetables. When she returned, the child was gone. She searched the yard and places around the hut but couldn't find him. He had to be found before Tommy came home or he'll kill her.

"Have you tried the neighbors?" Her mate asked. "Sorry I can't help search at the moment. After I complete my cooking, and if he's still missing, I'll help search if Tommy says so."

The latter came home drunk as usual. The minute he entered the hut, he staggered to a table where his meal awaited him. A look of pure bliss enveloped his face as he savored the rich peppery smells of the stew. He fished out a ball, with his fingers, and bit into it.

"Hmm-mm," he sighed his eyes rolling with delight, "This is why I love you; you haven't given me a son but you do know how to cook. Not like some people I know."

Soon, he was gulping down the food in earnest.

"Yahbom," he enthused, "this stew is good, delicious to be truthful. It's the best meal I have tasted in a long while. What meat is this?"

The question brought Yahbom and her girls from her bedroom.

"Monkey meat," she said, "I bought half a carcass from a hunter down by the river."

She watched as Tommy licked his lips then mixed some of the rice with a few fistfuls of stew. Her breath was held in check when he pushed a palm of the rice, topped by the largest meatball, yet, into his watering mouth.

His pleasure as he chomped on the food was a sight to behold. It stopped suddenly; he spat out the masticated food into the palm of his left hand. He must have bitten into something very hard; something that had him testing every tooth in his mouth.

Rubbery fingers then displaced the food from the center of his palm as he searched for the cause of his distress.

Immersed in the mixture of palm oil, rice, meat, and saliva was a partially chewed human thumb. The look on his face was one of loathing and disgust. He dumped the masticated food into the bowl of rice and stew. Three fingers went down his throat.

"What type of monkey was that?" He asked as the endeavor at vomiting failed. "How come it had a baby-like thumb?"

"A regular monkey," she said. "Monkeys have—"

Mariama burst into the room followed by her sister, Menna.

"Tommy," Mariama cried, "the baby is missing. Do you know where he might be?"

Tommy's eyes grew wider than saucers. They moved nervously from the face of one spouse to the other.

"My God," he shouted bursting into tears. "My God, Yahbom, that wasn't my boy? Tell me it wasn't my boy."

He got no answer: Her demeanor told the story.

As they watched, his face convulsed with pain and remorse. He pulled out clumps of his hair by their roots and dashed from the hut loudly uttering gibberish.

# Pa Brima's Tar Baby

Feathered wings beat desperately and, as if prearranged, a bevy of pesky birds rose up shrouded in a clock of brown earth.

"Allah, be merciful," prayed a disparate voice. Sweat poured from its owner's face and body to stain an already filthy gown. A gnarled hand wiped the face of the voice's owner, Pa Brima. "What a year? When not the birds, it was his other tormentors: Bra Rabbit and his family."

He looked over at his mate, Beindu, who stood a few feet away surveying the havoc the animals had done.

"Easy, now, dear," she said her hand protecting her eyes from the rays of a brilliant sun. "Remember your headache."

She loosened and retied her gara lappa then stooped resuming her task.

"Get our sons to keep out these pests." she said when her mate grumbled about not having help in ridding the farm of the animals. "Those boys eat us out of our food and home."

She smiled when her spouse retrieved a stone from a deerskin bag that hung from his shoulder. She prayed that he would kill whatever he was aiming at as he loaded the sling in his hands and let the stone fly.

Thunder-birds—anyone responsible for their deaths would in turn be killed by thunder and lightning—that were destroying a rice patch, one hundred feet away, scattered in a flurry of dazzling colors and dust to land a few seconds later.

The farmer studied the imprint of his wife's buttocks on her lappa as she bent over digging. His manhood quivered and he marveled at his good luck.

"Everyday I wake up I ask them to do just that," he said. "Do you see them around?"

"Kids, they think only of themselves at their age," Beindu said stamping her right foot, causing ripples to chase each other across her buttocks.

"What happen to the talisman you buy?"

The ripple parade fascinated him. If he didn't concentrate on the business on hand, he would have to take her here in the farm and he knew the rage that would elicit from her. He focused on a brown-baby rabbit feasting on a cassava patch.

"It was a waste of good money," he said. "These things don't work for me. There seems to be more pests in the farm after its use."

He threw a stick at the rabbit: It missed.

The bunny raised its head, sniffed the air then dashed off its antagonist's curses chasing after it.

His wife stopped weeding to ask if he had followed the witch-doctor's instructions exactly. If he had and it hadn't worked, he must visit him again. This time, he should ask for a stronger talisman: One that will work.

A warm feeling engulfed the husband. Watch out; watch out, he thought, you must control these erotic feelings: She hates it when you show them in a public place.

"I will do that," he said. "You know my thoughts about that man: He's a bully and a menace."

He joined her at the task of uprooting grass from a sweet-potato patch.

He dreaded facing the witch-doctor a third time over the matter. However, he left Wellington early the next morning for Hastings: Pa Musa's hometown. The approximately five mile walk was uneventful but a swirling mist had enveloped the newborn day by the time he arrived at his destination.

Five minutes of persistent knocking later, footsteps approached the front door.

"Sorry for waking you up so early, sir," he said to the man who opened it. "You are not angry with me for doing that?"

Pa Musa stretched then yawned like a feline.

"Why I be angry?" He asked a cunning smile on his face. "This is no problem to me: You go pay for waking me up."

He painstakingly wiped the sleep away from his eyes.

Generally, you couldn't tell what mood the witchdoctor was in so the visitor said that the talisman he made for his farm had not worked. Could he make something stronger: Something that would work this time around?

A huge fist struck him on the chin sending him to the floor; its owner towered over him demanding to know if he was condemning his workmanship. Was he saying he was a quack; he didn't know how to do his job? If it hadn't been that early in the morning and he hadn't said his prayers, as yet, he would have taught him a lesson he'd never forget.

"All I am saying is," the visitor said, "the last talisman didn't work. I may not have done all you said. I am sorry if I offended you. I'll gladly pay for another one."

His host calmed down. He helped him unto his feet then they both sat on the bench.

"That be the case," the former said, "I do my best job for you. I make something that go work. That be if you do what I tell you."

The visitor thought he'd escaped lightly this time around: People sometimes died after calling the witchdoctor names. He should watch out for what he said to him in their future encounters; there was no telling what he might do the next time. He asked if he should wait for the talisman.

Now standing and supported by the verandah's railing, Pa Musa grinned.

"So it be child play?" He asked his hands gripping the wooden structure. "If it be that easy, make it yourself."

He stuck out both hands with seven fingers raised.

"Come back in seven days," he said.

Backing away from the verandah Pa Brima made his way from the house. He could feel goose pimples all over his skin so he folded his caftan tightly around his person even though he knew they weren't from the chilly air. Seven days was too long a period to wait. By the time the replacement talisman was ready; his farm would have been destroyed by the damned animals. He couldn't have told the witchdoctor that; could he?

His doubts were real: The birds and rabbits decimated beds of cassava, rice, and sweet potato plants during this period. Only his fear of the witchdoctor's prowess kept him from paying an earlier visit.

On the stipulated visiting day, however, he awoke early and hurried to that worthy's house in Hastings.

"Want to make habit of this?" The owner asked as he stood shivering in the doorway. "I be happy if that be the case. This way, I make plenty money from you."

The animals had nearly eating him out of his farm since the last time he'd been at his house the visitor explained. He had to be that early so he could collect the new talisman and have it in place before going home at the end of the day. He approached his host and faced him. Why are his hands wrapped across his chest? He wondered. Don't tell me he is cold? Isn't he the witchdoctor?

"Come into the house," the home owner's voice broke into his thoughts. "We pray together and then have cups of hot coffee."

He grabbed him by his upper arms and tried pulling him into the house.

"No! No, thanks," the visitor said backing away. He then turned to grab the wooden verandah railing. "I have to be on my way to the farm," he continued. "My wife will be there waiting for me; you know what our wives are like this early in the mornings. Bring the talisman out and I'll leave."

His antagonist had, somehow, slipped between him and the railing and was pushing him, backwards, into the house. When they were finally in, he instructed his wife—an amused observer of the happenings—to prepare them some beverage.

Prayers were said while they waited, followed by instructions on the handling andplacement of the talisman in the farm.

"Why should no human eye see the talisman before it is set up?" He asked at the end of the instructions.

His adversary concentrated on rubbing his upper arm for a while.

"It wi—"

His spouse walked into the room with two steaming cups of coffee.

Rolling his cup between his hands, the visitor wished she would leave. To his consternation and dismay, she flopped onto a chair nearby.

"Go to your bedroom," Pa Musa ordered as he rose and marched out of the room. He returned toting an object wrapped in wads of banana leaves and bound with raffia. He demanded three hundred Leones as he slammed the talisman in front of the farmer.

The latter grudgingly handed over a fat wad of bank notes even though he thought the price was too high.

With the talisman on his head, he nervously walked away the words of the witchdoctor ringing in his ears.

He usually covered this distance from his farm in around two and a half hours. On this day, however, the journey took more than four. The talisman's weight increased, as time flew by, making his spindly legs wobble. By the journey's end, rivulets of sweat cascaded down his face to stain his all ready filthy caftan.

The talisman was gingerly set down when he arrived at the farm. He searched in his pocket, brought out a knife then cut away the leaves: A tarred-clay form was exposed. It was human with its arms extended out by its sides. It shimmered, ever so brightly, in the afternoon sunlight.

"I mustn't touch it," he said overcoming a strong urge to do just that. "The witchdoctor said that would destroy its powers. Nothing must stop me from ridding this farm of those damned animals."

He rummaged for something from under a pile of decaying grass. His hand came out with a hoe. Soon, he was digging a new bed for some cassava shoots.

The only break he took was when his mate arrived with his lunch. Since she didn't say anything about the talisman, he didn't venture any explanation either.

The blazing sun had begun its work by the time he'd eaten his lunch. From experience, gained by sometimes walking barefooted on tarred roads, he realized the tar's upper crust lay atop a hot mobile and sticky underbelly. To this, small pesky animals could be stuck and would not easily escape.

"Oh Allah, let this one work," he prayed as he walked home that evening.

His arms and legs listlessly hit Beindu and the mattress as they slept that night.

"No, not my potato patch," he screamed at one point. "Keep them from my potato patch, Allah. Kill these damned creatures before they wreck my farm."

The next slap to his mate's face awakened her. She noticed that he was in deep sleep so she lay quietly by his side. When a foot rammed into her stomach, however, she slapped him into consciousness.

"What is the matter, husband?" She asked. "Why do you toss so much in your sleep?"

He wouldn't let on he was having a nightmare about the animals in his farm. He told her everything was all right. In the morning, while on their way to the farm, he'll reveal all to her.

That journey was begun at the first light of day. It started with a jog which made Beindu and the boys, who loathed being up that early in the morning, annoyed. He had broken into a sprint that left his family straggling in his wake after only a few miles into this.

"Whoopee, it worked," they heard him shout as they panted their way up to where he stood about two hundred yards from the talisman. "He gave me something that finally worked. Allah be praised."

He stood in silence for a while then took to his heels in a mad dash for the talisman.

"Damn. My toes," he cried out: He'd kicked one of the talisman's legs.

Beindu asked what the matter was as she and their offspring came running toward the talisman. They found him cursing and hopping on one leg around the base of the talisman.

"He did it again," he shouted his face twisted in rage.

"Did what?" His mate gasped. "I don't see what you are complaining about."

She received a glare.

"Use your diseased eyes, woman," he said. "That Iguana-eater did it to me, again. When I get my hands on him, I—"

"You do what?" She asked.

"I'll kill him," he said concentrating on his foot. "I'll give his bones to the dogs."

They were all standing around the talisman now. What his spouse and offspring saw caused them to snigger. The mate tried controlling hers and failed. They developed into loud, rambunctious laughter that led to tears running down their faces and echoes resounding around the open spaces surrounding the farm.

"It did its job, huh? It caught some animals? Didn't it?" Beindu asked pulling herself together. "The witchdoctor promised it would, didn't he?"

Pa Brima looked balefully at his mate and hissed. She is right, he thought. He would need another day and a better trap to catch Bra Rabbit and his family. On the outstretched arms of the talisman, two rows of Thunderbirds—about thirteen each—had perched for the night. They would not be leaving at anytime that day or in the future. They were stuck to the Tar baby and were feebly trying to free themselves and fly away.

# Drunkard

Mrs. Osho pulled the huge, iron door open allowing a blast of cold Mount Aureole breeze into the house. Icy fingers of air grazed her exposed face and meandered through the sleeves of the pink cardigan she wore to chill her to the bones. She almost stepped on a figure lying, fetus-like, on the landing before noticing it. She took several steps backwards her mind racing. A second look, however, made her smile: She recognized the gently breathing form in front of her.

Something was wrong with the sleeping man, though. On a wound in his upper right arm, there was congealed blood. The flesh had been ripped open by the sharp, jagged edges of exposed bones.

"For God's sake, Barber," she said stooping and shaking the sleeper, "get up. You're courting pneumonia. What happened to your arm?"

The injured man groaned then stirred. Turning over to face her, he winced.

"I hurt bad, Missus," he said. "The pain kill me."

She rose and walked into the house.

"Christopher!" She called. "Come here this minute. Barber's hurt."

She listened to the slipper-shod feet on the staircase: They soon arrived at where she stood. A man in green pajama walked toward them: He shivered then wrapped his arm about his upper body.

"Hope this is important," he said. "This is my Day off: I'll like to spend it in bed."

He followed his wife's finger to the figure on the landing.

"What happened to you, Barber?" He asked standing over him. "You've got to see a doctor."

"It's nothing, Boss," the injured man said. "I walk on path coming up from Blackhall Road; the next thing I know, I am in the hole. I feel pain when I try to get out. That's all, Boss. There's nothing to it."

"He is stone drunk," Mrs. Osho said. "What a waste."

She knelt and helped her husband drag the blood covered body into the warmth of the kitchen then they busied themselves with removing his shirt and cleaning him up.

"You must take him to the hospital," she said after they'd examined the injury.

"I'd have come with you but we are in the middle of the Term's Tests. Take him to the Connaught Hospital, dear."

"The Cottage is nearer," her husband said. "He won't be attended to until after one in the afternoon at the Connaught."

"Just like a man," she said eyeing him coolly. "The Cottage is a maternity hospital. They don't cater for broken bones."

"I know that, Mrs. Know-all," he said. "Damn, there goes my Day off."

His wife's day was uneventful: She proctored three different examinations before she left for home. Her husband and their handyman had only returned about five minutes before she did.

"Did they fix Barber's arm?" she asked.

He said yes. He cursed everyone out at the outpatient. We

should have minded our business; the break would have healed a lot faster if he went to his medicine man.

"Think we should have another talk with him?" she asked.

"Who are we?" He asked. "Leave me out of this one, woman. I have had enough of him to last me a life time. Talk to him if you want, but leave me out of it."

She dumped her purse on the dinning room table.

"Nah," she said. "This time, we speak with him as a team. This is the third occasion this week he won't carry out his duties. He'll be off for at least a month. It would mean more work for the children and me."

He shook a graying head.

"Be stern, dear," he said. "Let him know you're the Boss. You don't need me for that?"

"I want you with me when I talk to him the next time. In his culture, women are not respected as they are in ours. Get a twelve year old boy to give him advice and he'll put it to practice. He won't if a woman does the same."

"In that case," he said, "take Olatunji with you he's about that age."

"You don't know when to be serious," she said hiding her annoyance. "I'll say it one more time; you come with me!"

The meeting should have taken place on the following Saturday: They found Barber stretched out—unconscious—on the cold cement floor of his one room apartment. He lay in a pool of his own vomit and urine. From his mouth wheezed a breath tainted with alcohol. Numerous pints containing liquids with bacterial and viral growths added to the nauseous smells in the room.

"Get up, Barber," Mr. Osho bellowed as he opened a window in the room then walked to the sleeping man to shake him by his unhurt shoulder. "Get up, man. What happened to his bed? I see; he was so drunk he couldn't get into it, huh?"

"Why ask me?" His wife said. She stooped to prize open the sleeping man's fingers from the bottle they grasped. "Jesus," she gasped handing over the container to her spouse, "it is seventy percent ethyl alcohol. It is marked 'POISON. NOT TO BE INGESTED.'"

He took the container.

"It should contain two hundred and fifty milliliters of alcohol," he said examining it. "This thing is controlled. Where did he get it? Wonder if he drank most of it?"

"We must assume he did," she said. "The more reason we must hurry him to the hospital: The time for asking questions will come later."

Her husband nodded.

"Don't leave the bottle behind," she continued. "They would want to know what he drank."

Her mate had grabbed the drunken man around the middle and with his employee's uninjured arm around his neck had begun walking to the door.

"I said you mustn't forget the container," she repeated. "How would they know what treatment to administer?"

"You're coming with us, right?" he asked.

She said yes.

"Bring along the container, then. There's nothing in it that'll kill you. Is there?"

"Olatunji," she called grabbing the bottle and stomping out of the room, "get a taxi while I change into some street clothes."

In another half hour, she came down. They were whisked off to the hospital in the waiting taxi.

"Hope it's the Children's we are going to?" Mr. Osho said while they were in the taxi. "They have the expertise to clean out people's digestive systems; they do it all the time on kids who swallow hazardous substances. And, it's just down the road. I want to be home for the soccer match on the radio."

"You don't care if he dies?" His spouse asked. "A man rolls on the ground and groans in pain and all you think about is soccer? Man, you're so insensitive."

He didn't see that it was any business of his. If the man deliberately drank bottled poison he should bare the consequences. He didn't buy him the alcohol. He didn't force it down his throat.

"Sorry," she said. "I got carried away. It's not easy to watch someone's life waste away. I am fed up with his actions but let's care for him for the last time. When he's well, we'll let him know he's no longer a child. He must take charge of his life."

He took her hands.

"That is okay," he said. "You must learn that certain things are beyond one's control. We have done the best we could: Supporting him through several binges; giving him a roof over his head, and salaried work. We can't help it if he keeps drinking himself into stupors."

"True, love," she said. "You know I hate giving up on people; I keep thinking there must be something I could do to change their lives. It hurts my feelings when I watch someone waste his life on alcohol."

Between her husband and the taxi-driver, the drunken man was manhandled into the Connaught Hospital building where he was hospitalized. He returned home after a two-day stay none the worse for the hospital imposed quarantine. He had an inkling of things to come when he was ordered to the main house instead of its occupants coming to his place.

"We've decided that you'll be paying your hospital bills yourself starting from the most recent," Mrs. Osho said. "We'll deduct two hundred and fifty leones per month for the next twenty four months. If at the end of that time, you incur any more expenses you'll be out of a job."

"Don't do that to me, Missus," Barber said. "My pay don't buy much ru—eh, I mean, food. Take away part of it, I starve to death."

"You won't," she said. "We won't be here always looking after you, picking up your expenses. We spend more on you than our children combined."

"Boss, please, talk to the Missus, for me," he pleaded. "Tell her I'll change; I'll give up drinking. If I get into another mess, I won't look to you for help."

"You have been given too many of those," Mr. Osho said shaking his head. "The past week alone we paid over five thousand Leones for your hospital bills: Money we could have spent on our children. No Barber, you have to pay your way from here on out." He rose and stalked out of the room.

They watched Barber one-handedly clean out the chicken runs and pig pens over the following days. During these chores, he sang, lustily, in his native Limba.

"Isn't he a changed man?" His Missus enthused to her husband and their Cook, Emma, after two weeks of his sobriety and industry. "Cook, please give him some food starting from today."

"He won't eat the food, Ma'am," Cook said. "He'll give it to anyone providing him with alcohol."

"Didn't we get off his case?" Mr. Osho asked. "Things will be fine for a week, or two more, it will then be back to normal for him."

His wife couldn't look him in the eyes.

"This is the longest he's gone without drinking," she said. "He should be couraged to kick the habit. Cook, don't you forget: He gets some food each day."

"He'll get it, Ma'am," Cook said. "It'll be like adding lipstick and powdering a female baboon with Talcum believing that that will make her look beautiful. He won't change: You're wasting time and money on him."

To which Mr. Osho said an Amen.

An uneventful second week flowed into a third. Barber worked harder with a plaster-of-Paris coated arm than with his two unbroken ones. His battle with the alcohol bottle seemed to be, if not practically over, in remission. On the twenty-eighth day of his abstinence, his Missus hardly walked into her house before Cook shouted, "Know what your son did today, Ma'am?"

She asked which of her four sons.

"None," she said. "I meant Barber."

"What did he do?" Mrs. Osho asked.

Cook busied herself with the preparation of the evening meal, ebbe'—a hotchpotch of cassava, yams, fish, onions, hot pepper, tomatoes, and palm oil. "He dismantled his bed and with the mattress took it to Pa Foday's carpentry shop."

"What did he do with it?"

Cook laughed. "He sold it off; he made a bundle. Bet we don't see him for a while."

"How do you know this?"

She'd followed him and hid behind the wall separating their property from Pa Foday's. She saw and heard the whole transaction: Hundreds of Leones changed hands.

"That amount of money, huh?" Their employer asked. "As you say, we won't be seeing him soon. If he is a no show tomorrow, he is dog meat."

He didn't show over the following two days. The family wasn't particularly worried: he'd been known to stay away for a week at a time. The situation continued until people he owed started calling on him, in person, for their monies. Everybody was at a loss as to what had transpired. The family began worrying when the Doyen of the bars, in the Kissy-Brook area, arrived wanting to know what happened to her favorite customer.

"No one knows," Mrs. Osho informed her. "Four days ago, he auctioned off his bed and mattress. We've not seen him since."

The Doyen laughed.

"That accounts for the money he had," she said. "He bought forty-leones worth of omole' (Gin). He and some other patrons consumed it all. He left another fifty in his account. Something must have happened to him. I don't see him leaving that amount of fire-water with me."

Mrs. Osho looked at Cook who stood nearby: They nodded.

"No, he won't," she said. "He's likely to drink himself into the grave than be done out of all that money. Wonder what became of him?"

The family instituted a thorough search, for their farmhand, that extended up the slopes of Mount Aureole to Fourah Bay College: He wasn't found. He'd been gone for over a week, when a foul, nauseating stench, of putrid flesh, pervaded the area. People grabbed their noses as they ran across a narrow bridge that spanned a stream in the path leading to the Osho's Blackhall Road farm.

Blame was put on the death of some animals (farm or otherwise). The sun was sinking in the sky two Saturdays away from the day Barber disappeared when the Oshos and several of their neighbors decided to solve the problem of the smell which now intruded into their very homes.

The search was a non-event; under the cement bridge over the stream, they found the decaying remains of a body. It was fully clothed. In one hand was a bottle with contents that had gone dark brown with dead insects floating in it. On its label were the just decipherable words: METHYL ALCOHOL; CH3OH. Ninety percent proof.

The corpse's drenched clothing had the larvae of numerous insects roaming at will: Their fat undulating bodies traversing it from head to toes.

From such a gruesome sight, Mr. Osho tried shielding his spouse.

"Let go of me," she said pushing him aside.

He could only watch her throw up as she approached the spectacle before them.

The corpse was eyeless seemingly accusing her of neglect. Through the sockets, myriad numbers of Soldier ants scurried over each other in their dash to get at the goodies within and the plump larvae that abounded on it.

A bevy of about a hundred ants hurried out of the right socket—as she watched—with what looked like pieces of lungs. Then, out of the hole representing the late nostrils, a mouse scuttled out pulling behind a long string of blotchy rotting intestine.

Screaming loudly, Mrs. Osho turned, grabbed her husband around the neck then went limp.

# Feigned Abuse

Nine-fifteen the display on the digital clock above a swing door said one hot and humid evening. Three overhead fans monotonously labored to dissipate the heat in Reception. Into the semi silence crashed the swing door bursting open. Through the halves, a young woman walked into the Reception area; she was a sight to behold: Jerri-curled hair dripped liquid over her light-complexioned face and the collar of her white cashmere top. A wide-eyed girl, about eighteen months, reposed at her right hip. Behind her, and almost hit by the halves of the door swinging to their positions of rest, trudged a whimpering male toddler clinging to her left arm like grim death.

As they drew closer to the front desk, so my anxiety increased: In an hour and forty-five or fifty minutes, I would be off work. I asked the lady if I could help when they got to me.

She smiled exposing a set of perfectly white teeth: Most of the women coming before me, for the first time, don't; usually, they cry. Her eyes had dark patches around them that made her face look blotchy.

A carry-all added considerable weight to her left side. It had the Brand name and price tag still on its handle. Something didn't fit: Why was she at the House? The women coming to us were usually, well, practically insane. They are disheveled, fear stricken, and many are sub-humans who cringe when spoken to. They don't appear with an expensive carry-all: Never having had one, or if they possessed one hadn't the time or inclination to throw things into it to bring along.

"Yes. Give me a room for three," she said.

I was intrigued by a voice that was by far too confident. It wasn't from somebody used to being knocked about and psychologically mistreated. Those women mostly whispered timidly. Their demeanor said they were hurting and did not trust their fellow human beings.

She let go the hand of the toddler who'd been fighting to free the same since they entered the office. She winced when the boy dashed to a rack and began tossing magazines unto the floor.

"Abiodun," her voice thundered across the hall, "stop that this minute. Come and stand by my side."

One more magazine flew to the floor; two tiny feet stomped on it then their owner ran to bury his face in his mother's gara-tied skirt. He burst out crying when she stooped, put her mouth to his right ear and whispered at length into it.

I suppressed a sigh. For a first encounter, she didn't show the physical signs of a victim of abuse. If she was psychologically affected, she was yet to display it. She didn't fit the battered-woman mold.

Two of our house-keepers had joined us and were listening to our discussion. By the looks on their faces, they shared my sentiments. One then wrinkled her nose and walked away.

I pulled out a drawer in my desk and took out a register: Several rooms were available so I handed her a form, in triplicate.

The daughter—who she still carried—was dumped on one of two chairs facing me. The carry-all went to the floor; she sat on the other chair and began filling the form. Minutes later, it was in my hands.

Mrs. Tamila Olusegun was her name. Her offspring were Abiodun and Thyra.

"My God, Abiodun," her voice suddenly rang out.

She bellows a lot, I thought looking up from the form to see the boy, forever on the go, rummaging among the objects on my desk.

"Behave yourself. Stand close to me."

The tiny hands of her angst were now on my stapler. They pulled it toward the child bringing along a cup containing an assortment of pens, pencils, and rubber bands to the edge of the table then to the floor.

The mother shrieked, stretched across her daughter, grabbed then pulled the boy toward her—across the little girl—and boxed him on the right ear.

He burst into tears.

She threatened to give him something to cry for then rose to pick up the things on the floor.

Battered women in my view (I am no expert) were usually bastions of defense for their offspring in a soured relationship. Mrs. Olusegun's conduct seemed otherwise.

"Will you be staying long?" I asked.

She continued replacing my writing equipment and rubber bands into their cup.

"A week," she said, "maybe longer." She raised her head. "I need a place to sort myself out then decide on my next move."

Straightening up, she plunked the cup on the desk then, with the sniffing boy tagging along, returned to her seat.

"Still married?" I asked thinking that someone should look out for the youngsters if they were not to be mistreated that night.

She shifted on her seat. The daughter in the meantime stood

on hers and with both hands pulled on her mother's right sleeve. They were gruffly thrust aside.

"Yes," the mother said to my question, "to an animal."

Look at who's talking, I thought.

We're trained to recognize the lapses shown by this woman. Such actions must be reported to the Council Authority. However, we couldn't in the present situation: This being the family's first visit to the House and they had arrived too late for any action to be taken by us. Also, our report could only be made in writing, in the morning, seeing that those responsible had all gone home for the day.

"Did your husband beat on you all?" I asked.

It was one question that was stipulated.

"Religiously," she answered.

"Does he know you are here?" The House-Keeper asked.

"Think I am stupid?" She replied. "He stormed out of the house after the abuse. He usually does and won't be back for two days, maybe, three. He always does that, too."

"Want my Daddy," the lisping voice of the boy cried out, startling me. I looked up: He had both hands, rolled into fists, rubbing his eyes. "Wanna go home, Mommy; wanna sleep on the four by Daddy."

His mother stood up.

"Look lady, you gotta find me something suitable for three," she said. "I will keep him quiet if we have a room to ourselves."

You would, too, I thought.

Meanwhile, the child continued to tug at her skirt.

"Wanna go home, Mommy. Wanna go home, now."

She tried pulling the garment from his tiny grip but to no avail. Finally, it came off to fall, limply, on the floor. Exposed was her shapely, light-skinned, and naked lower body.

"Drat! Now, you've done it," she said sending a backhander at the boy. "I'll teach you not to pull off my clothing." She reached for the kid's ears and violently twisted them.

The child wailed anew and was joined, a few minutes later, by his sibling. The lobby was soon in complete bedlam with the girl cringing away as the mother tried to silence her and the boy shouting, "Daddy, I want my Daddy. Wanna sleep by my Daddy on the four."

The situation brought me from behind my desk. I approached the whimpering boy who sat on the floor; he scuttled backwards as I tried picking him up.

"Don't cry," I coaxed when he was eventually in my arms. "Your Mom did tell you to stop; you mustn't take her skirt off in public." I held him close and patted his head.

Both hands were tightly wrapped around my neck, a wet cheek nestled against one of mine. His body shook violently wracked by heart-breaking sobs. The sobbing died down and he said weakly, "Daddy, I want my Daddy. Wanna sleep by my Daddy on the four."

This boy is obsessed with his father who must fear, or loath, his spouse to be sleeping on the floor, I thought putting the boy on one of the chairs to sit.

"Somebody shut him up," the mother yield addressing the counselors who'd congregated at Reception. "He'll drive me crazy if he keeps on saying those words. He believes his Dad is the cat's whiskers but he wasn't at home when we left. He doesn't understand the man's a monster: One who wants to spirit them away to that hell hole in Nigeria, Lagos."

It became clear: By her accent, she was an American. Her married name indicated she was the spouse of an African. These problems came up often: The husband wanting to return home (after his studies or whatever) with his family; the spouse absolutely refusing to go along. This made for bitter feuds: The husband becoming truculent as time to return home drew closer. At times, he'd threaten to kidnap the children he dearly loved. But many a time, it was the wife who absconded with their offspring never to be heard from again.

I had no sympathy for such women. They were married for better or worse. Who said going to Africa—with your spouse—was such a terrible thing? Most of the men, I understand, achieve prominent positions in their countries of origin. They somehow acquire the money for their spouses and children to visit America, on vacation, every so often.

If one should empathize with anyone, in this situation, it must be with the kids: They get caught in a tug-of-war between feuding adults. Through no fault of theirs, they go without a parent forever.

Unconsciously, I had walked back to my desk. I wondered if the kids should stay with their mother over night. It was passed ten thirty and, as I said earlier, the Social Workers had gone home by then. It took fifteen minutes to calm the boy down after which the family was placed in a room for four. As they struggled to the back of the building, the thought of the boy staying with his mother, overnight, continued to plague me. A few more hours with her, I felt, however, won't harm him.

"Don't wanna stay here, Mommy," he cried. "Wanna sleep in our house; wanna sleep on the four by Daddy, tonight." He repeated those words twice as he was dragged to the back of the building his right arm beckoning as if requesting help from me.

I was on my way home, in my Ford Escort, by eleven o'clock. The journey from my office on New Hampshire Avenue, to my apartment went pass White Oak Shopping Center then continued into Powder Mill Road; it takes ten minutes at that time of the day. Thoughts of the family filled this driving time.

At home, I took a hot bath then ate a cold-ham-on-rye

sandwich with lots of mayo, and drank a cup of cappuccino. While I listened to the soothing voice of Reba Macintyre, from my stereo I drifted to sleep.

I couldn't have slept for long. When I became conscious, it was one thirty in the morning. I staggered to bed where I dozed off until three o'clock. I woke up to find myself sitting up in bed my hairs standing on their ends. I was perspiring profusely and shouting, "Abiodun?" He'd been battered to death by his mother in my dream. The words he repeated the previous evening distressed me. I had to do something. What? I couldn't sleep after that.

Groggy, I arrived at the House at two fifty-five that afternoon. Walking into Reception, I met a bevy of grey-clad police officers.

"Ah-ha, here comes my replacement." The receptionist said.

The three police officers she spoke with turned to face me.

"She works the evening shift; she interviewed and placed the family when they arrived last evening."

My heart lurched; cold fingers ran up and down my spine.

"Are the kids all right?" I asked dreading her answer.

She took out her makeup kit and began doing up her face.

"Yup," she finally said. "Anyways, Lieutenant Bailldh thinks so. Talk to him, he's in charge of the men."

She shouted to a group of officers standing a few feet away,

"Lieutenant Bailldh, the evening relief is here, now. Come and grill her."

A not too tall man with black hair, graying at the temples, detached himself from that clique of officers and strutted over to ours.

Sandra, forever the flirt, beckoned at him with her head:

"Lieutenant Bailldh," she said, "Meet with Ms Clarkson. She has all the information you will need."

"Information he will need?" I asked. "She wrote the required information down on the form she filled."

"Indeed she did," he said. "However, there are certain things I would like for you to make clear: At what time did they all arrive?"

I thought for a while then said between nine-ten and nine-fifteen.

"Can't you be more precise?" he asked.

I said I couldn't. I had had a cup of coffee and was thinking that in an hour and forty-five or fifty minutes, or so, I would be on my way home when they walked in.

He turned away and stuck his hands into his coat pockets.

I relaxed then walked around the desk to the chair that Sandra vacated. The lieutenant swiveled around to face me, "Did she?" he started to say before realizing I wasn't there. "Oh, I thought you disappeared," he said after he'd placed me. "Was she excited? Was she overly distressed?"

"Excited?" I asked. "No. She was calm and calculated, too at ease for someone who claimed to be just abused. Distressed? Not the way she beat on the boy. The closest she was to that were the dark patches and puffiness around her eyes."

"You don't empathize with her plight?"

"I got the impression she was putting on an act," I said gazing into his face. "She was vibrant, not like a battered woman. She showed too much vitality for that."

"Explain, please," he said.

Pointing to the swing doors, I said that two types of women walked into our office:Genuinely battered women and the fakers. The former, after long periods of physical or psychological abuse, are withdrawn and subdued. They don't look us in the eyes: Maybe, they are generally afraid of people, or are ashamed of what the staff might think of them.

"Hmmm," he said then asked if I had anything else to say.

I said she exuded a lot of power and confidence. I couldn't imagine her not being in charge of any situation she was in, especially that of being abused. During her stay at the front desk, she dictated her wants to me. Also, battered women never came with their hair Jerri-curled, attired in crisp cashmere blouses and gara-tied skirts. Worst of all, she had that new carry-all to boot.

"Didn't all battered women beat on their offspring?" he asked.

A Social worker standing next to me said that most abused women were protective of their children who are, at times, mistreated by the spouse or boyfriend, too. In those cases, the misused woman acted as a buffer between her abuser and their kids, even though mostly unable to stand up for herself.

The Lieutenant pushed his hands into his coat pockets.

"What you're saying is most battered women would never knowingly harm their children?"

The social worker nodded her agreement. The mothering instincts of most women would be too strong for that to happen, she added.

"Did she hurt the boy?" I asked.

The Lieutenant shook his head. They disappeared, without a trace, overnight.

I thought that was impossible: She told me they would stay for a week, even longer. Something must have happened for them to disappear. Aloud, I wondered what it was.

Leaning forward, he peered into my face.

"After the events of last evening," he said, "she needed somewhere to pass away the night and pull herself together. She had to plan her next moves."

Why didn't she go to some relative or friend's house?

He shook his head and smiled.

"She couldn't under the circumstances," he said. "She realized those were the places the police would begin their search. This Home provided the ideal hideout: You would pity her so called predicament and not ask too many searching questions. Being with her young children would prevent you from turning her away so late in the evening."

She used our facility, I thought. I imagine she baled out of the House, early that morning, while the residents and night staff slept. She didn't care for the health of her kids only about escaping from her problems.

"Did she commit a crime before coming to us?" I asked.

The boy's words came to me with a vengeance, 'Wanna sleep by Daddy on the four."

"She murdered her husband," he said. "Their cleaning lady found his corpse this morning. He was on the bedroom floor; his head lay in a pool of blood that drenched the carpet. A terrible gash ran from ear to ear."

# A Brush with Death

Grandpa tamped the earth around the young coconut sapling he had transplanted on his ten-acre farm, off Blackhall Road, in the capital city of Sierra Leone. He stood up, brushed the soil from the knees of his pants in the fading evening light, and signaled his watchman and general help, Alpha, to pass the last sapling to be done for the day.

He smiled, his dusty right hand caressing his balding head as Alpha, after some deliberation, limped hesitantly toward the nursery muttering silently. He knew what troubled him: The farm, bordered on one side by a cemetery and on two others by a densely forested Mount Aureole, was a frightening place to be during the evenings. Wild animals wandered down from the mountain to attack those being husbanded. Also, on moonlit nights, ghosts were reportedly seen roaming among the coconut-and-grapefruit trees of the plantation.

Alpha had an unbridled love for his master. He tried to make him leave the farm before it became too dark. With his walking stick rapidly hitting the hard-packed earth, eyes alight, he would say:

"Boss, don't leave the farm so late in the evenings. Bad things pass for this place."

On these occasions, the master would smile to himself and think that his servant was neurotic. He wondered why he pressed so much on the matter and asked why he should leave early. Thoughtfully, he would concentrate on whatever he was doing then say, "I won't do that. I have never had problems going home from here."

Alpha now hobbled toward him with his stick in one hand and the sapling, held closely to his body, in the other. He handed over the latter then moved a few feet away to hop from one leg to the other, the stick going dub-dub on the sun baked earth.

"Boss," he said, "bad things happen here. The devil come to this farm."

Grandpa grabbed the sapling.

"What a lively imagination," he said dumping it into its designated hole. "What's all this nonsense about the devil being on my farm?"

He muttered as he carried out the transplant. At its end, he rose, dusted down himself then stalked up some steps leading to a farm house build on a knoll.

"Boss," his man painfully limped up the steps after him, "everybody around here know that the devil leave in this farm. I seen it with my two eyes by the stream."

Grandpa slammed the farm house door in his face.

For one crippled in both legs, the latter darted forward and used his stick as a wedge to keep it open.

"Keep out," Grandpa ordered. "I'm fed up with your fanciful stories. Next, you'll tell me that Allah resides in our neighbor's farm."

He busied himself with washing his face, neck, and arms at a wash basin then went on to change into his street clothes.

Alpha limped into the room and sat on a camp bed his chin resting on his stick's handle. He patiently watched while the other man dressed.

"It's true, Boss," he said finally. "Late in the evenings a big snake be at the goat pen."

The old man shuddered slowly releasing some of his angst. It was all in his imagination; he should behave like an adult and not tell lies, he told him.

"No, sir," Alpha replied a bit angrily. "I don' make this story up; there was a big snake by the goat pen three days ago. Other people, too, done seen it by the stream."

"I'm sure you all saw a snake," he said. "It had nothing to do with the devil; you people are funny that way: You see a puny worm in the twilight and think it's the devil."

A while later, "How big was this one anyway?"

He did not know for sure, the servant answered. It had been dark when he saw the snake by the slow-moving stream where the farm animals watered. However, he indicated a size of a foot-and-a-half in girth and twenty feet in length with his hands.

There was no way a snake that size could be in Freetown's vicinity, not with its volume of human and vehicular traffic, his employer said. Since he was fully dressed, he picked up a flashlight and his walking stick—as big as the non-business end of a baseball bat—and nodded his employee out.

He took the steps leading down from the farm house by twos then walked briskly to a wooded path that separated the goat and pig pens. This path lead from the farm to the main Blackhall Road and was infested with rain-dug potholes and ravines. At its top end, to his left, was a six-foot-high termite mound. This evening, it was under siege by a mobile sea of tropical Driver ants. These were attacking from their temporary bivouac in a near by underbrush.

He chuckled as he walked briskly down the path even though the evening was oppressively hot and the acrid smells of the pens assailed his nostrils. Alpha, he thought, was up to some mischief: For several weeks he had noticed that some of the animals, especially the goats, were going missing.

"Don't let him take you for a fool," Grandma had said when he'd discussed his servant's behavior with her. "Watch him closely: He's up to no good."

He'd agreed with her then and was certain about it now. He'd traveled halfway down the path, engrossed in his thoughts, before becoming aware of galloping hooves. They were followed by swift rustling noises from beyond the gently swaying underbrush that lined the path in the trees to his left. They came from the area of the goat pens that was some distance in front of him.

"I'll not stop nor get off this path, either," he said into the warm, humid evening his walking stick acting as a club.

The sounds relentlessly drew closer to the path; he recognized them as those of a four-footed animal chased by something large crawling over the dead leaves and shrubs on the ground. The closer they approached the more the muscles in his body revolted against him moving. His brain indicated he should stop and watch from a safe distance.

Oh, how he wished for something more potent than the stick he held. With a machete', he could do a lot better in his defense and very much so with a gun.

Out of the brush dashed a small kid goat bleating in fear; it leaped across the path as if all of Freetown were chasing it. In its wake appeared the swaying, flattened head of a black mamba, its tongue rapidly flicking out to smell the trail of its escaping prey.

"My God," Grandpa wondered, aloud, startled by the tongue's reach and the size of the head, "What'll the body be like?"

The reptile chased its prey implacably over the crackling leaves and shrubs, apparently without noticing him. Soon, it straddled the eight-foot-wide path.

"Where will it end?" He marveled.

He'd never seen one as big; it was about nine inches in girth and he could guess its length at more than twelve feet. Though not as large, as Alpha indicated, this was definitely the same reptile: Its scales were blackish green and shimmered in the moonlight like the reflection from a rippled stream.

He gingerly put out his walking stick and ran it along the portion of the animal still straddling the path. Heartbeat increasing, nostrils widening, he took in great gulps of air. He decided to have another go with the walking stick:

The reptile had almost gone across the path by then but on being stroked again, it doubled on its length to face him, its upper portion standing ramrod stiff. The large, flattened head swayed, threateningly, from side to side, seemingly wanting to grab its tormentor.

The latter stayed cool and held his ground as the forked tongue darted, in and out, as if to taste him, the unblinking eyes staring evilly at him.

By now, he held the walking stick at arm's length where it acted as a sword with which he jabbed at the incensed animal.

They eyed each other, across a divide of six, or seven feet; the old man was resolute in his determination not to give ground. The mamba became livid; it had lost its meal. Its antagonist saw the massive muscles contract. He held on more firmly to his stick.

Ever on the alert, he jumped backwards out of reach of the menacing head when the attack came suddenly. His weapon, however, was not so lucky it was swept from his hand like a matchstick and crushed to splinters. He realized the danger he'd placed himself. Not being a fool, he decided he'd lost this round.

He was certain there would be other rounds, with the reptile, in which he'd be better armed. He took several steps backward, turned and fled in the direction from which he came.

The python gave chase.

Nearing the termite mound, Grandpa veered right into the sea of Driver ants, scattering them in all directions.

Aieee-ee," he screamed as he ran through and felt the bites of those that attached themselves to his trousers and climbed up his legs.

The python, concentrating on the chase, wriggled headlong into the frenzied mass of infuriated ants.

The agitated invaders swarmed over its flicking tongue and into its mouth.

Alpha, in bed with his wife, heard Grandpa's screams and got up.

"Where are you off to? She asked as he hobbled away into the evening with the only lamp in their two-room home.

He didn't answer. He found his master under a huge mango tree. He was stack naked his feet stamping on the ground. The look on his face said it all.

The latter learned a lesson that evening: He didn't have a monopoly on knowledge. People like Alpha, though illiterate, had certain ingrained and natural abilities too. As he told Grandma, when he finally got home, a day later, he would listen to Alpha more often in their daily interactions. He would not dismiss his information as so much rubbish. If he had listened to him, the odds would have been in his favor during the encounter with the python.

"Next time," she said. "Next time."

# Unlawful Treatment

The king-sized bed in the Brownstone, in Beltsville, heaved massively then slowly settled down. Its occupant, Ernest, wondered at the lightness to his head; he felt like yawning; his face muscles refused to cooperate. The taste pervading his mouth was familiar; he was unable, however, to put a name to it.

He tried looking at the bedside clock; his head resisted the move. Savoring the sweetness in his mouth, he remembered where he had tasted the substance before: What was he doing at his dentist's? Several more efforts to move his head made it throb painfully making him want to retch. Through blurred eyes, he observed some movements to his far right; something, slowly, walked toward the bed then finally took shape: It was a woman's. She wore a white nurse's uniform, had a beautiful face, rampart brunette hair under a white cap, and moved about with leopard-like grace.

He should get her attention, he thought, as he watched her replace some objects from the bedside table, to his left, with one of his blue bowls. He beckoned with his hands; they wouldn't budge. His head, though a bit less misty, was still a ten-ton weight and the only external organs still functioning were his eyes and ears. The former became his mouthpiece when next she was close to him but they too failed to grab her attention.

"What's happening to me?" He asked watching his words form pictures then float upward. "Christ, am I going mad? Why am I in my bed and at my dentist's office at the same time? I shouldn't see him for the next six months."

He peered into the nurse's face: It wore a mask. What had he been doing, he wondered, before ending up half paralyzed in his own bed?

"Ah, yes," he said fascinated by his hanging words: "After taking a bath, I had a mug of hot cocoa then retired to bed; the next thing I knew, the numbness and sweet taste in my mouth."

"Wow, I administered six hundred milligrams of 0.5% diluted Novocain solution and he's still not completely under." The nurse said bringing him back to the present.

Surprising, he thought: Only two hundred milliliters of a 0.5% dilute solution, usually made his mouth numb at his dentist's.

"Maybe, he drinks heavily or he does drugs," a deep male voice said.

"No." Ernest watched his words explode out of his mouth to join the others floating in the air.

A person—in a white coat, cap, and face mask—walked up and bent over him. With bony fingers, he gently extended his eyelids then asked, "Nurse, he'll be sedated for the duration, huh?"

"Uh-huh," she replied. "You better hurry; dawdle, and you'll treat him without anesthetic. You know how painful that could be?"

"That wouldn't do? Would it?" White-coat asked as they laughed. "We want to do the work as painlessly as possible leaving his mouth immaculate and clean."

His words did nothing to reassure his patient.

"What's happening to me?" the latter asked. "Why is a dentist, and not a physician, seeing me at my home? One minute, Doctor? Come here, Nurse? Where am I?"

The only sounds getting to him were of instruments clanking against each other, and the nurse's voice humming softly.

"What if I am in an alien spaceship? God, will I ever see earth again?"

He lost the sounds of clanking instruments. They were replaced by two pairs of footsteps approaching his bedside. Through the haze, he searched their faces for something to remember them by as they stood by the bed; their masks prevented this.

"Hello, Ernest," White-coat said his mint-flavored breath caressing his face through the mask: He could still smell; the patient thought feeling some sense of relief.

"Yes, we know that much about you. I hope you are not afraid?"

"Of course, I am," Ernest said watching his words slowly making their way through the air.

"Did you say something, Ernest?" He asked and laughed. "Sorry we can't hear a word you say; your muscles are relaxed. You cannot move any but those of your eyes. If you must know, this is our contribution—Nurse and I—to humanity's welfare."

He bent over, parted the lifeless lips and peered at his patient's teeth.

"Most of you poor citizens are unwilling or unable to visit a dentist. Your oral problems are hidden until they get out of hand. Since you won't come to us, we are here instead: Isn't that thoughtful of us?"

He allowed a few seconds to pass then let go of the lip.

"See, you're a goner: Not a single muscular movement."

He picked up an instrument to force the orifice open; it

slipped between the lips to crash against the teeth. Finally, it broke through this barrier and its receptor saw the words, "Damn you, stop that: Leave my mouth alone," float upward to impinge on the masked face.

"Agh, someone with all thirty-two," White-coat cried. "Such buccal cavities are not normally seen in these parts."

"How would you know?" Ernest watched his words surround White-coat's face.

"Nice teeth. One blemish, though: This hole in the right molar the one next to the eye tooth."

"Crap," Ernest said. "My last dental check-up didn't turn up holes. Stop kidding around bozo."

He followed the man's hand as it stretched toward the nurse.

"How do we treat this one, Nurse?" White-coat asked. "Extraction isn't warranted. Drilling and filling? Uh-huh. He looks strong and should withstand the pain."

The nurse said; he was the boss. She was there only to hand over equipment.

"Spoil sport," he replied. "Hand me the drill."

"Heh," Ernest said, "leave my teeth alone." He watched his words float over his tormentor's head. "You can't break into my house and start playing the dentist with my teeth. Come Monday, I will see my regular dentist; I promise."

The thought of contracting the HI Virus or some other diseases, from the duo, caused him some consternation. However, he remembered; there were the sounds of hands being washed. Also, both wore surgery gloves.

He sighed when the dentist took the drill from the nurse. He watched the drill draw closer then slip between his lips; there were no cries as metal ground on enamel.

Something else slipped down his throat. Damn, he thought, it could be blood. I will choke to death.

Unimpeded by any resistance from the patient, White-coat worked expertly and quickly.

"There," his patient heard him say, "That's a job well done. I think I'll make this my life's work; won't you enjoy doing this for always, Nurse?"

"No, thank you," she replied. "I love being one with my bed, come nights. Where is the money in this?"

"Good for you, girl," their patient said watching his words rise merrily upward. "A beautiful dame like you should do something better for a pastime in the evenings. We could date, if it is the lack of a lover that makes you do this."

"Hand me the filling, please," White-coat said breaking into his patient's words. "This is the easy part," he added his mouth close to Ernest's ear. "Can you take it, my friend? I see; you are not one to complain, are you? You will take it like a man, huh?"

He meticulously began filling the hole.

"Don't you dare call me your friend," his patient said. "Friends don't do repair work on their buddy's teeth without their consent. I'll sue you two for every penny you have when I know who I am dealing with. When will this nonsense end?"

"Only a few more minutes to go and you'll have a perfect mouth," White-coat said as if reading his mind. "First though, there's a cleaning job to be done on these not so pearly whites of yours."

A cleaning instrument magically appeared in his hand. He pushed it into the pliant mouth; it vibrated against the excellent teeth removing plaque and stains from them.

"It's done," he said at last. "You have a set of near perfect teeth. You could be the envy of those nincompoops in Hollywood; Nurse, isn't that so?" He asked walking away from the bed.

"I'll pack the cases," she said above the sounds of running

water and his footsteps. "You carry on with the self-praising. Heh, where is the cleaning equipment?"

"On the bedside table," the shout came from the bathroom. "Be sure you collect all our instruments. We don't want to leave any behind for the police to find."

Metal clanged on metal followed by locks snapping shut. Some time later, White-coat stood by his bedside.

"We are leaving you now Ernest," he said. "In about four hours, the anesthetics will wear out. Some free advice: Keep doing the fine job on flossing and brushing. Get another toothbrush, though: The one in there's fit only for scrubbing the bathroom tiles; those sugary desserts, in the kitchen, dump them: They are injurious to your teeth."

He turned and marched out of the bedroom followed by the nurse who labored under the weight of the instrument cases.

The patient awakened the next morning to car-engines roaring into life and wheels screeching off into the distance. He attempted to stand up but fell back onto the bed. The third try had him planting unsteady feet on the floor and swaying, erratically, to the bathroom. His hands on the edge of the sink were white and trembling. He almost did not recognize the face in the mirror: drooping, red eyes; nostrils flaring taking in huge gulps of air, and shallow pale cheeks mimicking the face of an addicted drug binger.

"Wasn't it a dream?" He said his fingers mapping out the contour of his face. "There is only one way to be sure." He opened his mouth: Way back, on the right and in the middle of the molar before the eye tooth was a filling. "Who's gonna believe, when they hear this?" He asked. "They'll say it is an excuse for my missing work. I have to see my dentist."

"Are you sure; you didn't see another dentist?" His regular dentist asked when Ernest visited him that day. "I won't hold that against you; I'll only charge double my fees." With a tongue depressor, he examined his rival's work. "My, my," he said, "sure you didn't pay an arm and a leg for such a superb job? The work is excellent. Wonder what filling he used?"

"You don't recognize it, Doc?"

"No," he said. "One lives and learns each day." He waited patiently as Ernest hesitated before asking his next question.

"Think they were aliens, Doc? They did look weird in their white uniforms."

"What type of aliens, and from where?" He asked walking toward the faucet in the room. "The Dental Association of America has received such reports—twelve to date excluding yours—from the city's poorest neighborhoods where people cannot afford or don't have the time for proper dental care," he said over the noise of running water. "About two months ago, someone took up the responsibility of providing for their dental care. For all we know, he has done dozens more than have been reported. Maybe, he mistook your part of the city for one of those poor neighborhoods."

"Am I lucky or what. But how come you didn't detect the hole on my last visit?" he asked.

"When was that?" he asked going to a file display unit and searching. He brought out a file and skipped through. "The last time I saw you was over a year ago. That was time during which you could have lost all of your teeth."

"Doc, isn't my smile beautiful? Hope they apprehend them soon, though."

"Will you thank them for a job well done?"

Ernest smiled and twisted his jaw.

"You betcha," he said. "This sounds weird: It makes me mad and grateful at the same time. If they are ever caught, I'll thank them personally then cheer from the tallest building, in Bestville, when they get tossed into jail.

# An Unbreakable Marriage

Minerva ogled the push chair in front of the supermarket, along Krootown Road, in the west end of Freetown. She wondered how one could leave such a lovely baby amidst the noise of the hawkers, and the smell of decaying vegetables from the nearby local market. How she wanted to pat its curly head. She longed to have one of her own but David, her husband, protested whenever she brought up the subject:

"They couldn't start a family," he would say, "They were not financially strong."

She was still looking at the baby when its mother arrived, looked at her as if she were about to steal the child and pushed the chair away.

Their marriage had had a wonderful first year, she thought, as she walked to the parking area of the supermarket to collect her car. Of late, however, well, for close to a year now, David had lost interest in her as a woman.

Off handedly declining the offer of help—from a group of ten-to-twelve-year old boys—to carry her baggage, she asked herself why their marriage had gone sour.

"I'm the person I was two years ago: A Susu girl, beautiful and the woman he loved. Though almost twenty-two, I've still got curly, black hair atop a head with a round face, almond shaped eyes and a mouth that's almost always smiling."

She went to the back of her car, opened the trunk, put the groceries in, and absentmindedly closed it again.

"It could be another woman," she said getting into the car—a Mercedes 280E—and inserting the ignition key. "No. He doesn't seem to be interested in other women; he seems to be avoiding them completely. Is it money? I don't think so," she said starting the car: The engine stalled. "He makes good money as a junior manager in the 'Sierra Leone Diamond Corporation.' With the money I chip in from my dress making store, we are not in need."

The engine suddenly ignited and she took off.

"It could be his age," she said avoiding a group of women dancing in the middle of Wilkinson Road. "He is only twenty-three, at that age, men aren't supposed to have given up on their marital and sexual responsibilities."

On the coming Sunday, she decided, the longest period they were usually together, she would put some hard questions to him and hope to get answers to them.

The opportunity came as they sat in their living room that Sunday. She put the plate of food she ate from on a side table.

"What is the matter with me?" she asked. "Have I become an old hag? Do I have body odor? Why don't we make love any more?"

He continued playing with his plate of food.

"Neither, dear," he said. "You know what my job is like. By the time I get home, I am dog tired. I couldn't bring myself to do anything."

He watched her rise and walk to his chair.

"You are so tired even to hold me in your arms?" she asked.

"For more than a year, you haven't kissed me nor say words of endearment to me. Don't you love me any more?"

"Don't be silly, woman," he said putting down his plate. "I love you very much. These days, I'm preoccupied with certain things in my life."

She silently watched the red hues of the setting sun through an open window. A year was a long time for one to be preoccupied with things, she thought. Nothing should be so important to make a man ignore his wife that long.

"If I didn't know better," she said, "I'd say your preoccupation is another woman."

"What do you mean?" he asked towering over her. "Have you heard something? What are you talking about?

"I meant, I meant, you aren't really interested in other women." She'd touched him where he lived. "I recognize the way you look at and touch our male friends when they are around. That is not normal for a man."

"Go on. Don't stop now," he said. "I want to hear you out."

His hands clenched then un-clenched themselves by his sides.

She wiped a thin film of perspiration from her forehead.

"I'm married to one of the most handsome and well to do young men in town," she said knowing she was in deep waters. "All I do is stay home and think while he chases after other men in the evenings."

He slapped her—the very first in their marriage life—before she could move.

"Shut up, woman! What do you know about anything? Oh, God, what have I done? I didn't mean to hurt you dear. Please, please forgive me."

He must have been troubled by this for a long while, she thought. Wow! He'd never been this emotional before. She put an arm around his shoulders.

"Don't cry, dear" she said, "I know you didn't mean to hurt me. I saw your struggles during the past months. I want everything to be fine between us. What do you feel? When did it start?"

With his head on her shoulder he continued sobbing.

"It started long before we met, dear," he said. "I thought I was over it when I met you. Our marriage started gloriously but almost a year ago, the old feelings returned. These days, all I think of are men; we shouldn't have married. I'm sorry love."

"Don't say that," she said getting away from him—his fresh scent cologne was making her dizzy. She collected the plates from around the room and walked with them to the kitchen. "What have you done about it? Have you seen our doctor or a Psychiatrist?" I'll make an appointment for—next week—for you to see Dr. Roberts. Is that Okay?"

He followed her into the kitchen.

"I'll do that myself if you don't mind," he said. "I have some days off in two weeks: I'll telephone the doctor's office and make an appointment then."

Before they were married, she thought doing the dishes he'd taken her to great heights while they made love. She'd bragged about his prowess to her family and friends. What brought the reversion to his former state? Was it her fault? Had their love making become one dimensional and stale? Something must have changed in their relationship for him to go back to what he was. She hoped his visit to the doctor would provide some answers.

At this sage in the marriage, members of their families were becoming worried: They should have had a child by then, they thought. Some, mostly David's, thought that Minerva should see a Gynecologist arguing that the fault lay in a wife if a couple had no children. Her side of the family—with no belief in modern medicine—wanted them to see their favorite medicine men, from their respective villages, whom, they trusted and thought highly of.

At a party given by Minerva's youngest sister for one of her sons' first birthday, it was pandemonium when David's 'Favorite Aunt' asked Minerva, "When will you have a baby and call us to a happy occasion like this?"

Silence enveloped the sitting room and was broken by Mariatu, Minerva's oldest sister, saying, "That is no business of yours," as she matched the guilty Aunt's stare a pint of Star Beer and a plate of peppered chicken in her hands. "For all we know, it could be David who is incapable of having or is unwilling to have children."

'Favorite Aunt' adjusted the red lappa on her left shoulder and the wide brim straw hat over a pink and green stripped head-tie on her head.

"Utter rubbish," she said smiling. "The men in our family are prolific at having children: At least six each. I am sure David is no exception."

"In previous generations, yes," replied Mariatu. "You can't tell what the present generation is up to." She put her beer and plate of chicken down, got up from among her relatives and went over to face 'Favorite Aunt'. "Minerva will see your 'Woman Doctor' at any time. He will say she is fine; it is David who is impotent: An 'Okobo' man."

"For God's sake, that's enough!" Minerva shouted who, with David, had quietly listened to the argument going back and froth. "We would be grateful if you don't argue over us. I think we are old enough to decide if, and when, we want babies and not have them at your convenience and timing."

"It's your life and we realize that," 'Favorite Aunt' said straightening her lappa, yet again. "In our family, a marriage should be consummated within one or two years, topmost. You have been married for more than two years now; there are no signs of you being pregnant. Do you have problems we don't know about?"

"None that we couldn't take care of," Minerva barked. "And, as Mariatu said, 'it's our business.' Would you like to examine my pads, at the end of the month, from now on?"

'Favorite Aunt's mouth fell wide open.

"Sorry I interfered in your personal affairs; I thought I was helping," she said looking daggers at her. "If you have any difficulty, and you need advice, you could call on me."

She picked up her leather Kotuku (purse) from the floor and with two of her female relatives, in tow, flounced out of the house accompanied by the jeers of Minerva's.

"You hurt her feelings," David said in Minerva's ear. "Why were you so rude? You must apologize."

"In my own time," she said as her right foot tapped on the floor with the beat of the music being played. "You know what she's like." She got up, pulled him to his feet then dragged him to the dance floor.

"I adore her," she said over the noise of the music. "But, if I apologize now, she would think she had the upper hand this time, around. I would hate for her to feel so."

David kept his appointment with Dr. Roberts. A week later, he and Minerva had a lengthy discussion in which they decided to keep the marriage going. Not being sexually interested in her, it was decided that she could take a lover.

After months in agony and torment, she found one: He was the brother of one of her dress making customers. With her sexual needs catered for, she became more tolerant of her husband's preference.

Seven months after making her choice, she became listless, lethargic and complained of loss of appetite. There were severe bouts of vomiting and nausea in the early mornings.

These symptoms were explained to her mother who advised that she was pregnant.

She almost fainted. With disbelief, she matched her off to a drug store where a Pregnancy Test kit was purchased. It took restraint for her not to do the test in the car on their way back to her mother's.

She couldn't believe her eyes when the test was completed and there was coagulation. She peered at the instrument, shook it violently then examined it yet again.

"Yes," she screamed, "It is positive, Mom," she shouted leaping into the air.

She flung the instrument into the garbage can, hugged herself then vigorously rubbed her still flat stomach. Rushing out of the bathroom, she threw herself into her mother's arms and cried.

"I am going to love him, Mom," she said getting free from the embrace and walking to and gazing into a full length mirror. "In another month, he would show the first signs of life; oh, Mom, I am going to love him."

She caressed her breast then moved her hands to the bottom of her stomach to cup it. She went to the bed, and lay with her stomach on it and legs dangling over its side.

"Are you going to tell David about it when you get home?" her mother asked. "I should wait until after seeing the doctor, if I were you."

She'd waited for more than two years for this news; another three days wouldn't kill him, she thought agreeing with her. On the way home, she realized the import of her Mom's questions: When must she tell David about the pregnancy? And, more importantly, what would his reactions be?

"I may be in big trouble here," she said. "What would he say?" For all she knew, he may throw her out of their home.

She went to the refrigerator, on arriving home, took out some

Chinese food (Singapore Noodles) severed a small portion on a plate and plunked it into the microwave.

"Though he isn't sexually interested in me, in every other way, he has been a good husband. I know he would be hurt even though he gave me the idea in the first place."

She suddenly couldn't stand the smell of the food; she dumped it into the garbage.

"I'm all right," she answered on the Thursday morning of her visit to her Gynecologist. While waiting for that visit, she'd had bouts of vomiting in the early mornings much to her mate's concern.

'Dizzy Spells' were the excuse she gave when he found her holding on to a wall in the bathroom on this occasion.

"I made an appointment to see my doctor, today," she continued.

"Your General Practitioner or your Gynecologist?"

"My General Practitioner," she said

"Do you want me to pick you up at the shop and take you to him after work?"

"No, thank you. My appointment is for ten-thirty this morning. You would be busy then," she said.

"I will take that time off. It won't be a problem. I want to be there for you."

"I'll get one of the girls, at work, to drive me there," she said. I'll be all right. Don't worry."

She was promptly seen by her Gynecologist. A thorough examination ensued at the end of which the pregnancy was confirmed. She was given a list of things to-and-not-to-do in the coming weeks. She went home directly and waited for David to give him her good news.

She chose the moment when they watched a television discussion on the 'High Cost of Seeing Your Children through

College' to wonder what it would cost if she should have a child in about nine months.

David looked quizzically at her.

"Are you trying to tell me something?" he asked.

She continued staring at the TV.

"No," she finally said. "It was a hypothetical question."

"That cannot be true," he replied. "For days now, you have been behaving rather strangely: Feeling weak, nauseated and having morning sickness. These are all signs of early pregnancy. You hid it from me. Say it out, woman. What did the doctor tell you?"

"You won't be angry? She asked. You won't hurt me?"

He smiled but didn't reply. Minutes passed.

"I am still waiting," he said.

She was confused.

"I saw the doctor. After his examination, he said that—that—"

"That? What?" he asked quietly.

"I am four weeks pregnant."

She waited for him to rave at her, hit her, or stalk out of the house never to return.

He smiled then walked over to where she was, sat by her side and put an arm about her shoulder. "I knew that was the problem," he said. "Why didn't you tell me earlier on?"

"I thought you would become angry; thrown me out of the house. Truth be told, I would have hated that."

"Why would I have done that? I did encourage you in the matter of taking a lover. I expected you'd be intimate. If I was big enough to allow you a lover, I'm big enough, now, to face the consequences of my actions."

She looked into his eyes.

"Oh David, you are one of a kind," she said. "Not all husbands would take my news so sedately."

"I guess not," he said. "But, then, not every wife would take the news of my being gay the way you did. You helped me to the extent of wanting to make an appointment for me to see our doctor: You didn't abandon me when I came out of the closet to you. I could see that you desperately wanted a child: I couldn't give you one. In my own way, I did what I thought best for our marriage."

She snuggled closer to him.

"You are an angel," she said. "But, that was risky: What if I'd really fallen for him and decided to leave you?"

"Hmm-m-m, I don't know what I would have done," he said. "By the way, you are not madly in love with him? Are you?"

She smiled impishly.

"No," she said. "You and I are two of a kind and we love each other in our own ways. I am grateful for having you for a husband, dear. I really mean that."

# Painful Lessons

Jugular vein bulging and lips twitching Arnold watched his mate, Diana, step out of her shoes. Crass he thought: They will remain at that spot—just within the dinning room door—for the next three days.

When was she going to learn? She knew how he felt about apparels and things inappropriately left where visitors could see them. She was out to make him mad, it seemed. Weeks back, he'd spoken to her—in the privacy of their bedroom—about the matter only to be reminded they were co-owners of the house and that she had the right to do whatever she liked in it. He still chaffed at her admonition and thought about ways to force her into changing her reckless ways.

He bristled as she walked to the refrigerator to take out a bottle of ice-cold water and fill the glass she'd taken from the counter. Her butt was still nicely rounded he mused; how he would love to run his hands over it at this very moment. He smiled and shook his head: He had to concentrate on the matter at hand. Trouble was, he had no idea how to make his spouse and their offspring see things his way.

It started with the mother then made its way to the kids.

Mountains of assorted articles: Pairs of shoes; carrier bags; winter coats; book bags; other school paraphernalia, and purses with the fair sex's belongings, languished by the kitchen door, the first floor landing and that of the basement.

One would think they didn't have their individual bedrooms in which these items could be deposited. Theirs was a four-bedroom house: The largest room, on the second floor, was occupied by the wife and him. There were two other rooms on this floor: In the larger resided Seha, the daughter, and it was mostly well kept. The smaller they'd dubbed the Visitor's Room although it had a contingent of the wife's clothing, shoes, and assorted personal items cluttering it.

On the first floor was the drawing room cum dinning room from which led the kitchen. There was also a toilet for visitors, opposite the kitchen, down a short flight of steps and to your right going out of the front door of the house. From this floor led a staircase to the basement that was a finished apartment.

This was the domain of the son, Genus. It had a single bedroom, a bathroom, a sitting room with an electric fireplace, and a kitchen. A beige carpet graced its floor as it did the rest of the house.

When they moved into the house—in the early nineties—this apartment, with its antique-white-painted walls, was a beauty. It had been developed so the former owners could spend their evenings lazing about and enjoying its comforts. A brand new fireplace was installed just before the property changed hands and it gave warmth and a glow to the sitting room. Two years later, it was packed with electronic appliances (that should have been trashed) but no one, it seemed, had the time or the inclination to do so.

The bedroom had become a veritable obstacle course; one that needed agility to wade through broken down chest-ofdrawers which spewed out their innards, and boxes that vomited their contents of books onto its tiled floor. A computer stood on a wobbly table; underneath this were untold numbers of clothing and footwear which added to the colorful display on the floor.

Twice a year, at the least, one had to embark on a safari trek, through this jungle, on one's way to the boiler room that contained the water heater and air-conditioning systems to carry out their maintenance.

Arnold made sure he didn't frequent that basement apartment after the second year; the thought of the uses it could have been put enraged him.

Enhancing this rage were the daily occurrences: During spring, powdery pollens and mashed flowers were brought in, under foot, to leave ugly stains on the house carpet. It seemed the foot mats—on the landing before the front door and that after it, but before the carpeted steps leading into the sitting room area—were nonexistent.

Summer was no better: Dog poop from the streets; squashed fruits—shed by plum trees in their front yard—in untold numbers, and chewed gums made their way into the house and were crushed into the carpet.

You would think that the advent of autumn would bring some respite from the attacks; no, there were leaves to be trampled on then trailed into the home to carry out the assault. Then, it was the turn of snow, in the winter, to be marched indoors: This caused well-like, soggy patches between the dinning room and kitchen areas. They dried up leaving brilliant footwear patterns on the floor ornament.

It was an all-year-round assault by dress-shoes; jackboots; trainers; runners; walkers, and winter boots. Unsightly stains, ones that required the frantic and determined application of chemicals by professional cleaners, only, brought some relief to the poor, new, and hard-working floor decoration.

Its 'Part-owner' put up with the situation for years. On a Friday, about a week after the wife's birthday, in the month of December, in their fifth year of occupation of the home, he took action.

"When we arrive home in the evenings or whenever," he stated at the four-member summit he called, "can we go directly to our respective rooms to change from our street into our home clothes, then come down for dinner. That way, we won't make this first floor into our bedrooms. Besides, can we endeavor to wipe our shoes, thoroughly, on the rugs before and after the front door when coming into the house or leave them at the landing after the front door: It will prevent the sitting room carpet from being soiled and damaged with mud; pools of water; dog poop, and fruit stains: It's been on the floor for only five years but it seems as if wild animals have defecated and urinated on it. I will be grateful."

"What do you do when we come home from work?" Diana asked. "Nothing: I am as tired as you when I come home; yet, I have to prepare dinner. When I get to our bedroom, I am drained of all energy; the one thing I want to do is sleep. Money couldn't make me climb those steps twice, in an evening. I'll leave my things on the first floor until I have prepared dinner, eaten it, and partly digested it before climbing those steps to go to bed. If that gets to some people, so be it: They can take whatever action they think appropriate."

"It's not being tired that makes you leave your things on the sitting room floor for sometimes over a week," he said. If you are that tired, and are unable to go upstairs, when you arrive, you must at the least try and take them up with you when you go to bed or do so the very next day."

"Don't treat me like a child," she said glaring at the children who were giggling. "I never leave my things around on the first floor for more than a day; I know better than to do that."

"Our damaged carpets, that first floor landing, the kids and I know you do," he said laughing. "You've left several pairs of shoes on the first-floor landing, untold numbers of hats and scarves, displayed on its railing too, for weeks, before. Whenever I say something about it, you bite my head off. No dear, the children see your things on the sitting room floor, the landings, the kitchen and they think it is okay to leave theirs on them, too."

The man of the house was in purgatory over the following days. Also, to annoy him, flannel shirts, lightly-lined coats, hats, purses, and shoes were piled on both landings. Soon, these became hazards as one had to step through and, as they piled higher, over them to get to the basement.

Autumn coats, with heavier linings, soon made their way from room closets as the days got colder. They then decorated the banister leading down to the basement even when there was a coat closet just an arms-length away on the first floor landing.

Things left on this landing were tossed down the steps to the basement's landing, by Arnold, where they stayed for days, if not weeks: They would be trodden on and kicked about with impunity. When necessary, a book, a bag, some items of clothing would be retrieved and put into use (as-is) and, for whatever reason, returned to their same damned position later that day.

"Please," he pleaded when he at last got their attention, "put your things were they belong. It is annoying to come into the house and see your personal effects all over the floor when they could be easily put where they should be. What are visitors to think? You have rooms and whatever you do in them is your business: You can leave them as jumbled and messy as you like, even use the floor as a latrine and no one will be overly concerned. Let us keep this common area clean and tidy. I hate it when shortly before we're to get visitors, you people rush around trying to put things in order."

Efforts were indeed made to humor him over the next few days. Habits, however, die hard: A bitterly cold late autumn's evening saw them reverting to their sloppy ways. Action had to be taken he mused.

On a Monday, after a weekend in which things were left on the first floor landing since the preceding Friday, two pairs of wearable but smelly, thick, male socks went into the garbage bin. The Wednesday of the same week saw two hats and their matching fur-lined gloves going into a bundle that would finally make its way to a Charity Foundation.

Since no protests were made, a pair of perfectly new female Nike trainers walked its way into the ever growing Charity pile.

If the pair's disappearance or that of the other items, were noticed by anyone, heaven and that individual knew: However, since no one complained it became the turn of several opulent pullovers and many white-but-filthy undergarments, vests mostly, that'd have needed much effort, from the drycleaners, to get them to their original colors.

Things then progressed to totally presentable and wearable shirts, assorted colors, finding their way to the ever increasing bundle.

When a pair of perfectly tailored and well loved Eddie Bauer trousers—costing more than one could think possible—went missing did questions of the whereabouts of things arise. Suggestions that it might have been in its owner's bedroom were made; a thorough search of that edifice came about but the garment remained missing. Someone recalled seeing it on either the first floor landing, or that of the basement, during the two previous weeks: Those clotted areas were searched and partially cleaned out to no avail. Its owner thought he could have left it in his automobile but a rummage of the vehicle didn't turn up the article, either.

The final consensus was: Someone walked into the home and had the audacity to steal it. That very evening the landings were cleared out. They remained so for a whole week then the usual offenders were back on display aided and abated by winter coats hanging on the handrail leading down to the basement and matching boots standing guard on both landings.

Stuffs proceeded on their merry ways to the Charity bundle in a continuous and joyous stream. Soon, it was collected and a receipt issued for Income Tax purposes by the Foundation.

A new collection soon got started: A male, fur-lined, L.L. Bean half-winter coat being the first item to make its merry way into the bundle. Two days after being there, the mother, while searching for, as she later said, one of her favorite blouses discovered it. When it got there was anybody's guess although everyone had some inkling as to how and by whom. No one had stolen things from the home as they had supposed, he heard them saying among themselves; someone had deliberately disposed of things on the landings and everywhere else they shouldn't have been left in the first place: Everyone in the house knew who that 'Someone,' was.

The matter was never discussed in the open with that 'Someone,' though. On some days, things would be left on those landings until, well, late in the evenings. By bed time, however, they would have disappeared into their designated places or crammed out of sight in the cloak cupboard on the first floor landing. Deliberate efforts were now made to keep those landings clean and clear—as they were—when they first purchased the house.

Coming into the home, the boots and shoes, of the house's occupants, and their friends, could be heard laboriously being cleaned on both mats surrounding the front door. The floor carpet was now a joy to behold.

At last, lessons had been painfully but truly learned.

# Waylaying the Reaper

"Michael died from cardiac arrest. Michael died from cardiac arrest."

Words exploding, atomizing cells in the head of the deceased's fiancée. Back and froth they flew like tormented souls in Sally's distressed brain. She mustn't have heard the medic right; what in the world was he talking about? What cardiac arrest?

Her hands gripped the arms of the chair she sat in: The waiting room was now a swirling kaleidoscope of colors before her eyes. She rose, staggered to the medic, grabbed him by his narrow shoulders, and glared into his face.

"No, Doc., you are wrong," she said. "He came in to have kidney stones removed."

She followed the movements of the doctor as he removed his green surgery cap and white face mask. If she wasn't hurting so much, she would have laughed when the tape of the mask caught on his bat-like ears and he struggled to get it off. He must be one nervous wreck, she thought, watching him bundle the items into a ball which his fingers kneaded incessantly.

She didn't understand what he meant by: 'A valve of the heart malfunctioning and causing that organ to fail': Michael hadn't come in with a heart condition. Why weren't the standard tests done to ascertain that his heart was fine before the operation was attempted?

She came out of her reverie to hear him say he was sorry, yet again; they couldn't have done more under the circumstances. He then made an about turn and walked through the door marked "OPERATING-ROOM. KEEP OUT!"

The bereaved bristled: Could apologizing bring her fiancé back? She started after him but demurred to the restraining arms of a green-clad nurse. The tears cascading down her cheeks were brushed away.

"My fiancé is dead! She wailed. "What will I do without him? Oh, I wish I were dead too."

She received solace in the arms of her sister who stood nearby. She thought of the things they'd bought for their life together? Where had she gone wrong? Why didn't he wait until after they were married to die? Maybe, this was his way of dodging their being together. But Michael hadn't been that type of person, he'd have said something if he knew he had a heart condition. No, this was the fault of those damned medics.

Her sister rummaged in her purse then handed a handkerchief over.

She furiously dabbed at her face with it.

"You should start making preparations for Michael's funeral," the former said.

She couldn't, she replied. Not when Michael died at the hands of such incompetents. Medics were dimwits; she could strangle Michael's and his operating-room staff. She pushed her sister aside, turned, and dashed from the waiting-room screaming invectives in a loud but teary lament.

At the main entrance to Freetown's largest hospital, The Connaught, she stopped. She was perspiring profusely due to the afternoon sun. Her anguish over the death persisted but her anger at the medic had partially drained away.

She shouldn't have lashed out at the doctor? She thought leaning against the wrought-iron of the entry gate. People like him did a magnificent job each working day. She should know being a laboratory technician at the Cottage, a maternity hospital, in the east end of the town. Michael's death was just one of those mishaps; something that was destined to happen.

She began walking around the hospital's grounds. In the first few minutes, (time in which the rays of the sun slowly scorched away the last vestiges of her anger) an urge to see the face of her fiancé—before postmortem and embalming—became an all embracing thought.

The morgue was well known to her: During her years as student technician, she'd been in it on several occasions. Tissue samples from cadaver's stomachs; hearts; kidneys; skins, and other organs were collected and processed by her and other laboratory personnel. The slides and sections made from these were later investigated and used by pathologists in their quest in determining the cause of death.

Her long determined strides soon brought her to her destination. As a novice technician, she'd found such visits nerve-wracking. Several pathologists had told her that she would come to tolerate the smells and sights with time. She'd worked as a technician for nine years now and had never gotten used to the morgue's sights and smells. This time around, though, it was different: She had to see the remains of the man she'd loved before he was embalmed.

This process did awful things to corpses, she knew; it turned beautifully skinned individuals into dark leathery lumps of ebony. They are so dehumanized: You wouldn't recognize your mother after they were done with her.

An embalmed Michael would cause her much grief. She couldn't kiss him goodbye in that condition. Oh, how she yearned for his lips on hers. She would miss those voluptuous lips, the infectious laugh that cascaded from them. God, no longer would she touch his dimpled cheeks, nor see the twinkle in his eyes.

Her pace increased down the stairs to the basement that housed the morgue. On tip-toes she stole toward one of two doors with a "COLD-ROOM" sign written on them in red paint.

Making the sign of the cross, she approached one of the doors. Her guardian angel seemed on active duty: No one was around and the door had been left open. A sign that read, "KEEP OFF. NO ADMITTANCE TO NON-MORTUARY PERSONNEL," on the door didn't deter her from entering.

She entered a huge room with rows of numbered receptacles (whose silver-metal doors had clock like devices on them) along three walls. These rose up to the ceiling. A few were open and she could make out human shapes under what were once white sheets. Which one of them contained the remains of her, beloved, Michael? She wondered.

A metal table with various documents and several glass containers with body parts—brains; sets of teeth; livers, and eyes, all in rust colored fluids—carried a huge open ledger.

She nervously negotiated between trolleys (that carried deceased bodies covered up to their necks with dingy white sheets) to get to it. She was determined to discover the number of her sweetheart's receptacle.

The ledger was open at the page with the most recent entries: Michael Johnson's cadaver, although it had been entered, wasn't in a receptacle as yet.

Dingy coverings were removed, beginning with the trolleys nearest to the table, as she peered into faces that were grotesque in death. The pungent smells of body preserving fluids teased her nostrils making her want to sneeze and her eyes water. Half a dozen of these trolleys had been gone through before she came upon one whose occupant was completely uncovered.

She nervously approached: A cadaver, torso cut open, internal organs exposed, lay upon it. She screamed when several insect larvae scurried out of the displayed bowels. An offensive odor emerging from it added to the room's nauseating and revolting aroma nearly making her vomit.

Her urge to see Michael to kiss and cuddle him helped overcome these distractions. His cadaver surfaced another six trolleys from the one with the exposed body parts.

The heat hadn't impaired his remains as yet. He could be sleeping, she thought. He looked so serene: Michael with dimples frozen in death.

Touching his face made her shiver and it wasn't from it being cold. She reached for one of the clasped hands on his abdomen and began massaging it.

"Dear, dear, Michael, my love," she said tears pouring from her eyes to splash on their locked fingers. "I love you. Always will. I could sacrifice my career, all I possess, if that would bring you back, my love."

Her fingers, twining and entwining with his, had begun to adjust to the cold when they stopped. Had his moved? Desperately she resumed her stroking.

"God, please let it not be my imagination," she prayed raising the fingers of his left hand to her lips. She covered them with passionate kisses. Soon, both his hands were at her lips.

She dropped both and focused her kisses on his left cheek. When they elicited no significant response, her attention moved to his chest. Passionate kisses rained on his lips as she vigorously massaged that area.

Several faint, but unmistakable, thumps soon reached the ear she occasionally placed on his chest. They grew stronger with each successive placement.

Then, something cold touched the nape of her neck. Her head flew away from his chest: The offender was the corpse's right hand.

She opened her mouth but the scream didn't materialize. Leaping backwards, she steadied herself then dashed to the door leading out of the room her mouth wide open in what she still believed was a loud continuous scream. She couldn't hear the sounds, though. All she experienced was her chest expanding and contracting as she inhaled and exhaled.

Sweat poured from her body to soil the armpits of her dress as she slowed down then stopped on reaching the bottom of the stairs leading up from the basement.

Wasn't that Michael the love of her life? Wasn't he the one she wanted to give her life up for a few minutes back? Why was she running from him then?

She made an about face, hurried from the steps and back to the room to face whatever awaited her.

Michael was sitting up on the trolley, his body shaking like a leaf in a gale. On his face was a look of utter bewilderment.

She nervously approached him.

He asked, if the operation was a success. What was he doing in the morgue instead of a hospital ward? Why was she looking so flustered? Had she been running?

"Oh, Michael, my love," she cried overcoming her fears and falling into his arms, "I had given you up for dead: A cardiac arrest case."

She shivered as her hands caressed his ice-cold frame.

"God, in his mercy, has given you back to me. I'll worship him until the day I die."

She kissed him: Waves of blood coursed through her veins to

explode in her brain even though she was trembling from the cold.

Searching a metal cabinet against the fourth wall of the room produced some white coats several of which were perfect fits for him. Her first attempt at getting him off the table failed: He seemed to have gained weight since he came in for the operation. Maybe, this was the dead weight people spoke about so much. But, love gave her the strength to bring him to the floor. He couldn't move his limbs so a metal chair standing by the table (with the documents and body parts) became his resting place. Then she was rushing out of the room one more time.

"Help, get a doctor," she cried taking the steps upstairs by twos. "Man comes back from the dead. He now freezes in the ice-cold mortuary."

An hour later, she stood by Michael's bedside in the Extension wards. Dr. Bucknor—looking sheepish—was by her side.

"How did the operation go, doc.?" The patient asked. "Was the procedure a success? Why am I so cold?"

The operation wasn't completed the medic said and he was feeling cold because he'd spent nearly a day in the mortuary.

"I died?" he asked.

The medic said he and his other doctors thought so that morning. However, it was nice to see they were wrong.

"I see," he said. "I wondered what that magnificent place I was in could be. Its citizens wouldn't have me: Something about me being too young. It wasn't my time to be there. I still had something important to do before I left earth."

He was alive because of Sally the medic told him. If it wasn't for her love, he wouldn't be on a hospital bed.

"It was comforting to know one was loved that much," the patient said.

His arm reached out, encircled Sally's neck and pulled her head down to his mouth.

"I love you," he whispered. "I'll be indebted to you, for the rest of my life, seeing you brought me back from the grave."

"I couldn't let you escape that easily," she answered. "Not when we were so close to saying our marriage vows. Remember, you promised to be my spouse in another month. There was no way you were getting out of that. I could have sold my soul to the devil to hold you to your promise."

# Taming the Cat

Mom looked up from her book, THE SORROWS OF SATAN, to the cat by her side.

"Up Kitty, what did we do today?" She patted her lap and smiled.

The cat meowed softly then jumped onto the lap and curled into a ball. With Mom's hand absentmindedly stroking her glossy black coat, she purred contentedly, licked her paws then closed her eyes.

She opened them, when raucous laughter reached our ears; they came from kids sliding down Kissy Road on their naked behinds, on the tar mark road, under the rain.

I used to enjoy that type of fun; one could feel the raindrops splatter on ones hot face then roll down to caress and cool ones body as one slid down slopes in the road. This however, caused bruises on our bums which became infected and took a long while to heal.

Remembering the beatings I received, from my parents, on such occasions, and it alone, kept me in doors on this one.

Life wasn't always this idyllic in our home as depicted by the situation in the drawing room. In the two years that Daniela, my older sister, became shanghaied by Kitty—then about a month old—our lives had become hectic.

Long and savage fights between the darned cat and my pet, Old-man, were the norm until my dog died in a collision with a car. Now, it seems that without him to fight, the feline vented her anger on the furniture particularly Mom's cushions in the drawing-room.

"Get out! Get out you vandal," she'd shout, "Look at my lovely furniture. What happened to it?"

Her fury on getting home and finding shredded white feathers and stripped materials over highly polished furniture and floor sent the family scampering.

On these occasions, four in all, since Old-man died, Kitty's shrieks were vociferous; her back would arch its hairs standing erect. Strutting like Monroe, she would make her way down steps leading into a cellar. Before merging with the darkness, she would turn to give her antagonist who always stood at the top of the staircase, a look of royal disdain.

The fifth occasion was no different: I didn't expect to see the dumb cat for the next three days. My sister, the cat lover, stood by Mom at the top of the stairs and cooed.

"Kitty, darling, come out from that nasty black hole; come out, and your only friend will soothe your feelings."

Five minutes of these entreaties passed and then I heard Dad say,

"Live the darned animal down there if that's what she wants. I hope the mice gang up on her and she becomes their food."

"Don't say that, Dad!" Daniela said stamping across the none-carpeted wooden floor. "She understands what people say about her; Mom did hurt her feelings."

I cared less; if she liked, she could stay in that cellar forever. That was not to be, however: On the third day, she surfaced with satisfied purring and the grooming of her glossy coat to progress up the stairway like a Prima Donna. She even looked plumper than when she went into that hell hole.

"Meow, meow," she cried dogging Mom around over the following days. Her tail would always be high as she rubbed her fur against Mom's legs. Mom reciprocated by throwing her portions of the food she prepared. Sometimes, she even stooped to stroke the black form.

These truces were, usually, short lived. A week after Kitty's reappearance we arrived home and, as usual, Mom was the first to go into the drawing-room.

"My God, look at what that alley cat did to my room," she cried.

I listened to the rain beating a marching melody on the corrugated-iron roofing of the house before hurrying with Dad and my sibling, to see the damage: Everyone knew that Mom was testy on rainy days but the room was sure in a shambles.

"Wow, did Kitty really do that?" Daniela asked as she knelt to inspect some shredded feathers.

Mom looked at her for a long while.

"Who do you think did it?" she asked. "When I get my hands on that cat, I will murder the monster." She kicked at a mole-hill of stripped-floral material on the floor.

"Look at what she did to my settee; my beautiful settee," she said as we watched the feathers float back to the floor. "I'll strangle that cat." She tore at her hair now. "When I—" She began but fell silent.

Dad had walked over and put an arm about her shoulders. He told her not to be so angry and exited.

Mom shrugged the arm away.

"Christopher," she said to me, "Help your Dad search for the vermin. Daniela, get her cage; that devil leaves this house today."

Sis's face crumbled.

"Mom, you can't do that," she said. "You can't send her away. Who'll care for her?"

Mom shrugged.

"She goes to the pound," she said fingering a jagged tear in the settee. "There or somewhere she will not be this destructive."

Daniela walked up to her and took both her hands.

"Give her a last chance, Mom," she said her eyes pleading with Dad.

Mom didn't buy that. She's had too many last chances; if she stays in this house, tonight, I will move out. You won't see me until she leaves. She focused on Dad for a while then marched off in the direction of the staircase to the cellar, we all followed her.

In my eight years of living, this was the second time I would be down that black hole.

The air smelled of cat's urine and damp. I huddled closer to Dad, as he cleared various objects blocking our way, and we continued to the far end of the cellar.

"Here, Kitty. Where are you, Kitty?" he called. "Come to Papa, my pet." We waited, but she did not show. "Kitty—" Dad began.

"Stop that racket." Mom shouted directly behind me and made me jump. "She knows we are here. Christopher, stand by the door."

I flew to the door, closed and stood just outside of it.

"Don't fight me," I heard Dad say as the cat screeched when at last she was caught about fifteen minutes later. "She warned you not to shred the furniture again; you had to have your way."

The culprit's owner waited at the top of the stairs cage in hand. She watched, as Kitty, protesting vehemently, got shoved into it.

"What happens now, Dad?" she asked

We all watched Dad for a while.

"Ask your mother, dear," he finally said walking to the bathroom. "Me, I'll clean myself up."

"She goes to Grandpa's farm," Mom said after he'd gone into the bathroom.

Everyone knew what that meant: Grandpa's farm was a desolate, snake-infested place about four miles from our house. The darned animal wouldn't stand a chance against the larger and wilder creatures that roamed it: Although it would have lots of smaller animals to feed on.

"Not that, Mom," my sister protested. "She will be eaten alive." She ran to Dad as he exited the bathroom. "Dad, do something, please," she begged. "My poor cat will die from exposure to the rain at the least."

Her eyes welled as Dad walked to a window and looked out onto the street.

"Think about the time of day, dear," he said. "It's raining; it's very dark for six in the evening; it will take some time to get to the farm, and come back, on foot."

Mom strolled, leisurely, to their bedroom door.

"You had better be going, then," she said turning to look at us. "The longer you dawdle the darker it'd be on your return journey. The rain will not cease just for you."

She flashed a smile: Dad had turned from the window.

"Coming, Christopher?" he asked.

Now, I wouldn't miss Kitty's abandonment for all the Cadbury's Fruit & Nuts in the world and I loved those damn things. I grabbed the cage from Daniela and, with my raincoat over my head, rushed after him.

It took about forty-five minutes, at Dad's pace, to get there. As it had turned dark, when we arrived, I stayed as closely to him as I could shaking uncontrollably as we approached the small, white-painted farm house on a knoll.

Dad snatched Kitty's cage from me and putting his face near it said, "Sorry Kitty dear. I guess you needed some more house training. It was our fault."

I looked around as something moved into a clump of grapefruit trees.

"Let her go, Dad," I said my eyes peering into the darkness. "You know that is not true: Mom put her in obedience school, two different times."

Dad told me to be quiet.

I did but imagined that slithering sounds came from the brushes to our right.

"Dad, can we go home?" I asked. "Something is moving in the brushes."

He looked down at me.

"Oh, all right, Mama's boy," he said and opened the cage.

Kitty, with hisses and snarls, sprang out and disappeared into the night.

"Don't blame your mother for sending Kitty away," Dad told Daniela when he noticed she avoided Mom, two days later.

She said she did; she hated her; she shouldn't have sent Kitty to the farm. The poor cat would die of fright out there. It was the first time she was alone in the wild.

Dad took her by the shoulders and held her at arm's length.

"True, dear, but we are the ones who pay for the repairs. Care to contribute the allowance you receive during the next year?"

He received a withering look from his daughter who then hurried to both front and back doors to find their porches empty: She found them empty over the next three for her, I would think, harrowing days.

However, Mom—the life and soul of our evening's activities—had gone silent over this period. She sat in her favorite chair with a book open before her, at times staring into space, her right hand stroking an invisible something on her lap.

"Sit down!" she snapped on the fourth day of Kitty's exile when Sis started on a trip to the front door. "Sit. Don't you have any school work to do?"

The object of her rage stopped in mid-stride to slowly turn and face her.

"You witch. I hate you; I really hate you. Wish you could drop dead." She stormed out of the room.

Mom threw her book on the side table by her side and made as if to go after her.

Dad stepped in between them.

"Let her go, dear," he said. "She's distraught. Give her a few more days and she'll come around to our viewpoint."

The powers that be decreed that due to the torrential rainfall, the following day, there would be no school, or work but for the Essential Services.

Daniela and I settled down to breakfast while looking forward to a day of leisure. We were blithely into a game of Scrabble—Mom insisted—in the drawing room, when some noises came from the front door;

I pretended not to hear them.

They persisted, becoming more frenetic as the minutes passed.

"Won't you see what is causing that noise?" She asked.

"What noise?"

She said the noise sounding like something scratching on the front door.

I listened for a while then said I thought I had heard a cat's meow.

"You are only saying that to torment me," she said.

"It is okay by me," I said. "See if I care."

Whatever stood out in the rain did not intend to give up now.

"Meow, meow," it cried with renewed vigor.

The chips in her hands flew every which way as she jumped to her feet and tore toward the front door; this she flung open allowing a drizzle of rain to drench me where I sat.

"Kitty, darling," she screamed, "Is it really you?" Stooping down she grabbed something from the porch and hastily closed the door.

In her arms, a fluffy-ball in black cried pathetically as they marched toward me. Weak gargled noises came from within the wretched feline. She purred once and tried to lift her head but it fell back onto her mistress' arms

"You poor thing," the mistress cooed breezing in the direction of the bathroom. "Wild animals couldn't get you, so Mom prayed for rain. Don't shiver so; I'll take care of you; I'll protect you from her in futu—" Her voice trailed away.

"Keep her away from my drawing room for the next few weeks, Daniela," Mom said watching us, with Dad, from their bedroom's doorway. "We have decided to seclude that area from the rest of the house."

My sibling's eyes almost fell from their sockets.

"Will you do that for Kitty and I, Mom?" she asked.

Mom said yes.

"That darned cat grows on you," she said. "I missed her too, dear." She extended her arms and Sis rushed into them—wet feline and all.

"Sorry about yesterday, Mom," she said. "I shouldn't have called you a witch and said that I hated you. I don't seem able to control my temper and tongue at times."

Mom said that was okay. They had to work on her temper but there was plenty of time to do so starting at that very moment.

While they still held on to each other, I turned to Dad.

"Is that all the punishment she gets?" I asked him. "Aren't some people lucky? Bet, if it were me, Old-man would be in the pound, and I in his dog-house for months if not years."